T0329411

The Sirius Squad 3: Planet Wars

By Khulekani Magubane

Illustration by Thobani Gambushe

Photography by Lotte Manicom

umSinsi Press
PO Box 28129
Malvern
4055
Kwa-Zulu Natal
South Africa
www.dancingpencils.co.za

ISBN 978-1-4309-0112-9

This novel is *original and all views expressed in the book reflect the author's beliefs. The opinions and views expressed are not those of **umSinsi Press**. We are an independent publishing company whose sacred objective is to provide budding authors with a platform from which their voices can be heard. We believe in publishing information and view-points of different cultures and from different perspectives, in fairness and recognition of our country's wonderful diversity.*

Rest in peace, Bab' PQ. Rest in peace, Miriam. Rest in peace, Xaba. Rest in peace, Snqobile. We miss you. Thank you for everything. In honour of Boseman, Eshgedom, Tom, Simmons, Poitier, and Tate.

Thank you, TQ. This trilogy would not be the same without you..

Previously on *The Sirius Squad: Earth's Last Defence* and *The Sirius Squad: Between Enemy Lines...*

In The Sirius Squad: Earth's Last Defence, Menzi Gumede learns that he is not just an ordinary boy from KwaZulu Natal, but an alien from an ancient race called the Nommo of Nibiru in the Sirius star system.

Upon learning this, he also finds out that he was sent to earth as a defender against intergalactic tyranny. The discovery of his true origins coincides with the rise of a new threat to the natural order of the universe.

Menzi is befriended by Mogoma, a Nommo soldier from Nibiru. Through this new friendship, Menzi is thrust into an exciting, high-stakes adventure. Mogoma tells Menzi that an alien race known as the Mathra is on their way to earth to find an artifact called the Positive Logos.

When combined with the Negative Logos, the Positive Logos unlocks cosmic power over the universe and all matter. The Mathra hope to combine the Negative Logos with the Positive Logos to destroy the colonial Andromedan Empire, the entire universe, and recreate it with the Mathra as its rulers.

1

Menzi finds himself among the Nommo soldiers as an ally with the brutal Andromedan Empire on a mission to prevent the Mathra from getting their claws on the Positive Logos. Menzi meets characters like the pacifist Pleiadian Taheeq and the hard-headed Andromedan princess Innozia.

In an attempted siege by the Mathra, Menzi and the others see the Positive Logos' intense power for themselves. The Positive Logos (which has inexplicably taken the form of a human baby) sent a sonic blast at an attacking Mathra fleet, forcing them into retreat.

After warding off an attack from the Mathra, the Andromedan forces and the Nommo hide out in a lagoon to plot a strategy. They keep the Positive Logos safe from the clutches of the Mathra and their leader, the Architect.

In The Sirius Squad 2: Between Enemy Lines, the Mathra resort to trying to smoke out the Andromedan and Nommo militia by levitating the entire landmass of the east coast of South Africa thousands of feet in the air with a forcefield and conducting a search for the Positive Logos.

Meanwhile, in Andromedople, Princess Innozia's mother Queen Oyo is asked about her empire's involvement in the mission to stop the Mathra and she expressed no interest in keeping the Positive and Negative Logos for herself or conquering the whole universe in that way.

However, her younger daughter Princess Natiki said she believed it was the destiny of the Andromedan Empire to seize the Positive Logos as well as the Negative Logos and use the two artifacts to bring the entire universe under Andromedan control.

Natiki secretly masterminds her own mother's assassination and claims the throne over the Andromedan Empire in her older sister's absence. She then raises her militia and heads out to get the Positive Logos and the Negative Logos for herself.

Back on earth Menzi's brother, Nathi, is trapped in the city of Durban, which is encased in the forcefield that the Mathra created to search for and find the Positive Logos.

With his resourcefulness and sheer grit, he manages to help innocent people escape a part of the city that was seized and patrolled by Mathra foot soldiers.

Meanwhile, Menzi, Mogoma, Innozia, and the rest of the heroes decide to emerge from their lagoon hideout to confront the Mathra in a fight. The Mathra are successfully outgunned in aerial battle after Menzi successfully summons the legendary water beast Mazomba to defeat the Mathra fleet.

However, the win is a pyrrhic victory, and Menzi, Mogoma, and the Positive Logos are captured by the Mathra mothership and surrounded by Mathra servants. Natiki advances onto planet Nibiru to find out more about the Logos from the elder leader of the Nommo, Elder Amma.

Will Menzi and his friends succeed? Will the Mathra get their hands on the Positive Logos and wipe out all other life in the universe to create their own cosmic, dystopian hell? Will Princess Natiki make a universal dictatorship out of all living things? Find out now in The Sirius Squad 3: Planet Wars.

Prologue

"We need more warriors soon, sent from the stars, sun, and the moon..." – Nasir Jones, 2001. ible)

Location: Planet Nibiru, Sirius star system

Like a true backdrop of tranquillity, the planet Nibiru looked as picturesque as ever. The two white suns in the sky lit up the distant world constantly. Waves from the wall-to-wall oceans on the planet's surface roared and crashed into each other, as the small network of floating islands drifted gently in the breeze.

The newly coronated Andromedan Queen Natiki looked at the strange world around her with curiosity and a touch of smug hubris. She looked at the mysterious plant life that included flowers that grew meters high then broke off of their stems to float to the atmosphere in an evolutionary bid to get more energy from the two Sirius system stars.

Glorious and fantastic creatures most imaginations could not conjure flew the skies of the planet adorned in unreal textures and colours that did not even have a name. The water on the planet had a silver, shiny quality to it like alloy or soldering iron.

Natiki looked down at the ground she stood on. Her soldiers stood on either side behind her, holding their weapons at the ready. She squatted down and cupped a handful of sand in her palm. The sand on the floating island where she stood shone like silver glitter.

Elder Amma – the matriarch of the Nommo – looked at Natiki with a stoic smile on her face. Natiki fixed her face and flung the sand out of her hand. She looked up at Elder Amma to see the ageless mother of the Nommo smiling at her. The princess stood upright. "It's beautiful, isn't it?" Amma asked.

"It's dreadfully dull and cold," Natiki answered as she looked around at the alien world around her. She walked closer towards Elder Amma. "Unfortunately, I'm not here to talk to you about pretty beach views and flowers," the princess said as she stood in front of the Nommo elder.

Even for a planet covered with wall-to-wall oceans and a few floating islands – where the only intelligent life lived underwater – the planet Nibiru had a haunting silence to it. The whistling wind and crashing waves were the only sound to be heard for a long distance on dry land.

Two suns shone as bright as ever in the Sirius star system, causing everything on the surface of Nibiru to cast two perpendicular shadows; a short one that squatted beneath its object and a longer one that stretched away as if it hoped to escape.

The sky had a grey, almost metallic colour to it. Even the water glowed like solder under the light of two suns. The silence and tranquillity of the environment did not give away even the subtlest hint of the ominous occasion that Nibiru was about to find itself in.

The two were completely surrounded by their respective servants, but the numbers did nothing to break the tension. Elder Amma was surrounded by Nommo warriors ready to protect her. Natiki was flanked by Andromedan soldiers with a similar charge to protect their new queen.

Elder Amma walked over to a strange plant that resembled a tree stump and took a seat on it. She turned to Queen Natiki, who had not moved from the moment she walked up to the mother of all Nommo. Amma smiled at Natiki again and the new Andromedan queen kept a stoic scowl.

The wind blew the fine orange tendrils on Queen Natiki's head this way and that, but she continued staring at Amma, unfazed and emotionless. A small spring spouted water next to Amma, from the ground of the island that the two were standing on.

Amma cupped her hand and reached for a handful of water. She drank the water out of her cupped palm and beamed a soft smile. Her attention turned back to Natiki who took a few steps closer to the elder.

"I heard your mother passed away, young princess. The people of Nibiru pass on our sincerest condolences. Grieving a parent can never be easy, even for a royal who stands to inherit an intergalactic empire. But that's not why you're here, is it?" said Amma.

"First of all, I am now the Queen of Andromeda. I was crowned, as is my right, fairly recently. No matter, though. I will not hold the misnomer against you for long. I suspect you won't regret it for too long either, in any event," Natiki quipped.

"Succession is decided rather quickly over at Andromeda these days, isn't it? I remember when your mother took over the reins from her own mother, Queen Sabursa. It was after a much-delayed memorial," Amma said.

"Like you said, ancient one. That is not the reason why I am here. Do your abilities include mindreading or shall I explain myself further?" Natiki asked as she raised her right hand until it was directly in front of her face and clenched it into a fist.

The Nommo warriors tasked with protecting Elder Amma inched closer to Natiki and her Andromedan militia. The queen's soldiers, in turn, raised their weapons and aimed the Nommo with laser blades humming and ready to fire. Ultimately, none launched a salvo.

Elder Amma smiled at the avaricious princess. "Natiki, why so angry? You practically have the cosmos at your fingertips and here you are, in a sanctuary of monks and their spiritual leader, asking for more from those who have nothing compared to you," Amma inquired.

Natiki scowled at Elder Amma as the look on the princess' face turned from stunning offense to disgust. She turned her face to her right and spat to the ground. She turned her gaze back to Elder Amma and drew her laser blade out of its scabbard.

Natiki ignited the laser blade and pointed it in Elder Amma's direction. The Nommo warriors that accompanied their elder murmured amongst themselves nervously. Waves crashed as shining droplets danced between the stares that the Andromedan princess and Nommo elder exchanged.

"I believe you are confusing anger with resolve, old lady. Unlike my mother and my sister, I know what must be done for the ultimate benefit of my people and my empire. It is time that every civilisation in the universe chooses a side. On one side we have Andromeda and all of its pliant allies. On the other side, we have all of Andromeda's enemies. There is no longer any room for neutrality in my universe. Those who even fraternise with our enemies will grow sympathetic to their hateful vengeance. They may even give safe lodging to our enemies and be excited by their fervour to rise up against us as well. My mother and my sister were too weak to do what their empire needed them to do. But you will soon learn that I am not Queen Oyo Seviv, and I am not Princess Innozia. I am Queen Natiki. Now, I ask you who you are! Are you a friend of the Andromedan empire or are you a foe?" Natiki asked.

Elder Amma smiled as the red light beamed from Natiki's laser blade. She shifted her stance until her hind legs were all the way erect, adding another three feet to her height. Natiki stepped back, ready to engage as she looked up at the elder.

The change in Amma's stature was an impressive feat that might have weakened the resolve of a lesser warrior, but Natiki would not be so easily intimidated.

"You will learn that my peaceful predisposition is far from a show of weakness, young princess. I do not answer to the charge of friend or foe, much less to colonisers. But one thing I am is a tough, old lady who refuses to be pushed around," Amma declared.

The Nommo elder stretched her hands out and above her head as sharp, blade-like bones protruded out of her elbows and forearms. Her eyes went from a warm look to a serpentine glare. Her skin immediately hardened into rough, metallic scales.

"Fine! Have it your way! If you will not grant me your peace, obedience, and servitude, then I will settle for your cold, dead silence. You have been warned!" Natiki warned, her laser blade still pointed at Amma.

Natiki pounded her fist against her chest, prompting her armour to shapeshift for battle and form a helmet over her head. She raised her laser blade to strike Amma, but the elder of the Nommo gave the Andromedan a swift roundhouse kick, sending her flying back twenty feet out.

11

Natiki hit the ground, unharmed but enraged that she was hit, a sign that she had not been in battle in a long time. Her laser blade lay a few feet away from her. She got back on her feet, but as soon as she looked up, Elder Amma was flying at her with a strong tackle that took her back down to the ground.

A fight immediately broke out between the hundreds of Nommo warriors guarding Amma and the thousands of Andromedan imperial troops that accompanied Natiki to Nibiru. Andromedans pulled out their laser blades while the Nommo warriors drew their lightning daggers.

Some of the Nommo warriors served swift kicks and electric strikes to the Andromedans while the troops of Andromeda hit the Nommo with cuts and blasts from their laser blades. The Nommo yelled a war cry as they continued to attack the Andromedans and hold off their assaults.

Amma attempted to hold Natiki to the ground. Her strength was vast, but the Nommo elder had foolishly left herself open to attack. Seizing the opportunity, Natiki unleashed a barrage of punches on the elder's face.

Opting to create some distance between herself and the elder, Natiki pushed Amma up with her legs, sending the Nommo elder flipping over and falling on her back.

Natiki immediately rolled over and grabbed her laser blade. She got to both feet and fidgeted frantically to get the laser blade lit up again. Once it illuminated, she pointed it in Amma's direction, looking to fire a shot. Amma was already charging at her by the time she aimed.

Amma gave Natiki a swift swipe with her right arm and a blade on her forearm struck Natiki. She fell back but fired three shots at Amma from her laser blade. Three bright red beams shot out of the laser blade and hit Elder Amma, deterring her momentarily, but doing little further damage to the ageless being.

Natiki got up to her feet again and kept firing. Amma found her rhythm and managed to swipe each of the shots away with her forearms. Her arms were singed by the shots from the laser blade, but her wounds healed moments after they appeared.

"I see you are looking to do more than just draw blood," Amma said as she slowly walked towards Natiki. A green glow came out of Elder Amma's eyes as she used her telekinetic abilities to pull a boulder out of the ground. Natiki panted as she watched the levitating boulder rise and slowly cast a shadow over her.

The boulder hovered in the air behind Elder Amma, surrounded by an aura that glowed the same green that was emanating from her eyes. Natiki slammed her hands together with one loud, strong clap.

A red aura surrounded the princess, and her armour grew another spikey layer above the golden armour she was already wearing. An added bazooka-like weapon that could function from reading her thoughts appeared on Natiki's left arm, with a network of cables connected to her arm.

The shoulder pads on Natiki's new armour had a network of thousands of fine spikes and shimmered a blinding gold that was so bright that it was easy not to notice that the armour had the Andromedan insignia engraved on every part of it.

"You can't stop me, old hag," Natiki hissed as she stared at the Nommo elder. Amma stared back with her glowing green eyes as she levitated with a twenty-foot boulder floating a short distance behind her.

"And you can't make me kneel, princess," Amma retorted. The elder raised her arms as if to call the boulder's attention to follow her instructions. She waved her arms down swiftly and the boulder went flying in Natiki's direction.

A courageous and indomitable Natiki flew directly in the direction of the massive boulder that was also hurtling in her direction. As she collided with the object, she activated her new bazooka-like weapon — which was an Andromedan matter warping cannon.

The energy from the cannon hit the boulder with a force that was so direct that it punched a hole that was slightly larger than Natiki was right through it. The boulder was enveloped with red light before it shattered into thousands of pieces.

Where the boulder was moments ago, Natiki stood in mid-air, letting out a hellish, vengeful scream. She aimed her matter warping cannon in Elder Amma's direction and fired a shot. The fast and agile Amma jumped out of the way of the shot, which darted into the horizon, pushing land and water out of its radius for kilometres.

Amma jumped straight at Natiki and hit her with a knee to the gut. She followed with four successive punches to the head, sending Natiki flying to the ground. Natiki landed on her feet, crouching, and looking up at the Nommo Elder with an enraged stare.

Amma turned to her right as she floated in the air. She saw twelve Andromedan soldiers springing forward to attack her with their laser blades out. Her eyes glowed green again as she gestured an open palm in their direction.

Suddenly, gigantic vine-like structures emerged from the ground of the island they had gathered on. These vines rose from the ground to grab all twelve of the Andromedan soldiers that were charging at Amma. They wrapped themselves around the soldiers and dragged them down to the ground.

The Andromedan soldiers screamed for help. They frantically shot at the vines and cut at them as they struggled to break free of their grip. But the vines would either absorb the damage from the laser blades or regenerate from any damage they sustained instantly.

Once the Andromedan soldiers were back on the ground, the vines did not stop there. The vines continued to drag them into the ground. The Andromedan soldiers screamed as they were being buried alive. The ground closed up and swallowed them, ending their screams.

A startled Natiki looked around her as she realised what had just happened to the twelve soldiers. She pushed a button on her right wrist. Moments after, a golden board whizzed in her direction from the Andromedan mothership. Natiki jumped so that she was now standing on the flying board.

Amma turned to Natiki and chastised her out of sympathy: "I take it you are now coming to the inconvenient realisation that you did not provoke a bunch of pushovers. This does not have to end in tragedy for you, young woman. Leave us in peace and go home. Chart a new way for the Andromedans."

"Never!" Natiki yelled. "I have come too far! I am too close to the manifestation of my destiny to turn back now! I will not be denied of what is mine! Do you think I will be intimidated by magic tricks? What is it that you just did anyway? What jungle voodoo is this?!" Natiki demanded to know.

"Poor child," Amma replied. "Did you not realise the moment that you landed on this planet? Did your mother not tell you about me? Or did you not pay attention to her wisdom. I am the physical consciousness of the very planet you are on. I am Nibiru and Nibiru is me."

"Shut up!" Natiki shouted in desperate rage. She charged at Elder Amma with her hovering board. "I don't care what you are! You will acknowledge me as your ruler, or you will pay for your defiance to my authority with your very life!"

Elder Amma's eyes glowed green again. Dark clouds gathered in the Nibiru sky. The rumble of thunder in the distance got closer to the battlefield. Bolts of lightning flashed around Amma as she levitated in mid-air.

Amma raised her right arm and vines emerged from the ground of the island to pursue Natiki before she got to the Nommo elder. Natiki dodged the vines, blasting at any of them that got closer enough to her to drag her underground and suffocate her with soil.

One of the vines managed to reach Natiki from behind and wrapped itself around her left leg. She tried to struggle out of its grasp, but the grip only got tighter. The vine began to tug downward and Natiki could feel herself losing balance on her hovering board.

Natiki grabbed on the vine and tried to pry herself loose from its grip. More vines emerged and wrapped themselves around her arms and her right leg. With each firm tug, she could feel herself descending gradually.

Natiki finally resorted to using her matter warping cannon on the vines. She raised her fist and allowed it to charge up. She then rammed it against one of the vines and the vine disintegrated into dust. She fired at the remaining vines and they, too, turned to dust and fell away.

As relieved as Natiki was to avoid getting buried alive, she only took a quick sigh and immediately shifted her attention back to Elder Amma. She charged at the Nommo elder at full speed, raising her matter warping cannon as bright red sparks flew out of it.

Elder Amma took a defensive stance. As soon as Natiki got to the Nommo elder to deal a blow, lightning flashed between the two of them. The force of the flash pushed them right back apart. Natiki charged at Amma again on her hovering board.

The Andromedan soldiers struggled to muster an advantage over the Nommo warriors that they were fighting. While Amma fought Natiki, she was also able

19

to telepathically call on the forces of Nibiru's ecosystem to the aid of the Nommo warriors at the same time.

Some of the Andromedan soldiers managed to summon their own hovering boards to float away from attacking Nommo. They could also evade the elements of the planet that they learned could be used against them as weapons.

Amma managed to dodge a barrage of strikes from Natiki. The elder summoned lightning to come from the sky and strike Natiki. Black thunderclouds mixed in the sky as thunder rumbled louder than before. A lightning bolt formed and made its way to Natiki.

As the lightning made its way to Natiki, she quickly made a bid to counter it with a blast from her matter warping cannon. As the lightning struck the Andromedan royal, blinding sparks flew from her body. She let out a scream as she shifted her matter warping cannon in Amma's direction.

The light from the matter warping cannon appeared to steer the energy of the lightning bolt away from Natiki and towards Amma. The elder was hit with a combination of the cannon's beam and the lightning straight from Nibiru's skies.

Amma was sent hurtling to the ground. She fell hard on a nearby cliff. Almost immediately, the weather around the battlefield improved as the dark clouds scattered and the rumbling of thunder subsided.

Natiki flew down to the spot on the cliff where Amma had crash landed. She found Amma lying on the ground, scorched, wounded, and lying in the rubble. The elder of the Nommo had been dealt a heavy blow indeed.

Amma was lying on her side. She slowly shifted her position until she was on her back when she realised that Natiki was floating above her. Natiki had a stoic look on her face and a cold stare in her eyes. Elder Amma looked up at her and smiled.

"I have to say, I am impressed. More than just a pampered princess. You are a formidable fighter," Amma strained, coughing between every few syllables. The Nommo elder pushed herself up with her arms until she was sitting up.

Natiki looked down at the ancient Nommo elder with a slight hint of pity and a hefty dose of disdain. She tapped on her chest with her right hand. Her matter warping cannon receded into her armour, which in turn changed back to its less spikey, more regal, and ceremonial form.

"It's over, Elder Amma. If we keep fighting, I will kill you. While I do not have any qualms about doing just that, I am of the view that you are a lot more useful to me with your breath still in your lungs. Now tell me; how do I use the Logos? What do I do when I have both the Positive and Negative Logos?" Natiki asked.

Amma rested her back against a rock so that she was sitting up as she looked at Natiki. She grimaced through the pain as her femur protruded out of her right leg. The elder was also covered in dirt and her own blood.

"You're wrong, princess. There is no scenario in this misadventure where you win. Regardless of what happens, you will lose something. But what is harder; losing a battle to conquer the universe or losing your mind when the power you amass drives you beyond the limits of your own sanity?" Amma groaned.

Natiki seethed. "I thought you were smarter than this, elder," she laughed softly to herself. "When I say something will happen, it tends to happen, regardless of how anyone around me feels about it. So, are you going to cooperate, or am I going to have to figure this out by myself? Because I can, and I will," Natiki warned.

"You're...you're not..." Amma strained. The Nommo elder coughed up blood. "Your heart fights for hollow glory. The others seeking the Logos are stronger than me. The Nommo that are aiding your sister are united. Even The Architect's destructive vengeance is more substantial than your vain megalomania," Amma said.

Natiki laughed out loud and slowly clapped, mocking the pious high priestess of Nibiru. "Very nice! Spicy. I like it. Now do you have any last words?" she asked as she ignited her laser blade and aimed it at Amma.

Amma looked at Natiki and strained a half smile. "Oh yes. I have some last words," the elder said as she placed her fingers to her temple. "Remember Yasuke! Remember Queen Nzinga! Remember Mansa Musa!" Amma screamed as her eyes glowed green one more time.

She suddenly swiped her left arm to the right. A vine sprang from the foliage to Natiki's right to attack her. The Andromedan princess quickly drew her laser blade and shot Amma's last ditch attack down. Natiki immediately sprang to Amma's body.

A large, long blade protruded from the Natiki's fist. She grabbed Amma by her head and drove the blade into her throat. With three hard, violent twists Natiki decapitated Amma. The elder of the Nommo and planet Nibiru was dead.

Natiki's battle armour receded completely until it was only her imperial, ceremonial armour that she had on. She drew in a deep, sombre breath as she stood up, Elder Amma's severed head still in her hand. She looked around her as small embers of fire began to eat at the plant life around her.

Natiki hopped on her hovering board and flew off of the cliff. Back at the shore of the floating island, her soldiers managed to overpower the Nommo warriors, after the death of their mother caused them too much anguish to allow them to keep fighting.

She landed her hovering board among her soldiers. "What happened up there, Your Majesty?" asked one soldier. "We noticed a change in the environment, and we immediately gained the advantage on..." the soldier immediately stopped asking questions as soon as he saw Amma's severed head in Natiki's hand.

The other soldiers looked around them and saw fires raging in the distance. The planet suddenly became cold and dark. The shore of the floating island was strewn with the bodies of dead Nommo warriors. Natiki raised Amma's head over her own. The soldiers immediately kneeled before her.

"My soldiers. Remember this day. This is a moment that will live on forever in the history of Andromeda. More than a fable, fairy tale or myth. This is the day that Andromeda grows from an empire to the absolute power of the universe! Now we head to the distant Sol Star System to get the Positive and Negative Logos. Once we do that, we destroy all of our enemies. With the power of the Logos, we will establish ourselves as the supreme power over the entire cosmos with me as your queen," Natiki declared.

"And what about Princess Innozia?" asked one soldier.

The occasion suddenly grew even more tense, as soldiers waited to hear the instructions of their new queen where it relates to her own sister.

"As far as I am concerned, she is as good as a fugitive of Andromedan justice. She has no authority over you as Andromedan soldiers. But if you are skittish about meting out justice to her, don't worry. I have every intention of dealing with my sister myself," Natiki said.

Murmurs came from the soldiers, confused about what Natiki had meant by her promise to deal with Princess Innozia.

"Does anybody have a problem with anything that I have just said?!" Natiki asked, daring any of her soldiers to challenge her.

The soldiers fell silent. She looked at them, still kneeling with their heads facing the ground, looking for the slightest hint of defiance.

"Good!" she said as she started walking towards the mothership. "Now run me a hot shower, please? Queen Natiki has a universe to conquer..."

Chapter 1: The End Begins

Location: Earth, on the Mathra mothership

The darkness of the room gave Menzi and Mogoma no reliable way of gauging its size by sight alone. The only light that could be seen came from inexplicable sparks in the distance that looked like lightning and the bright red glow that beamed from the eyes of Mathra Carpenters that surrounded Menzi and Mogoma.

The two Nommo warriors stood back-to-back, each in their Nommo armour. Menzi was carrying the Positive Logos in his arms and the more experienced Nommo warrior, Mogoma, was armed and ready to defend them from the inevitable onslaught of the Mathra.

Mogoma attempted to contact the other soldiers in the Andromedan army to alert them that he and Menzi had been captured by the Mathra with the Positive Logos still in their possession. He frantically pressed on a communications device on the chest plate of his Andromedan armour.

"Andromeda, can you hear me. We are on enemy grounds with the Positive Logos in our possession. The situation is dire. Please relay instructions or send assistance. I repeat, please relay instructions or send assistance," Mogoma said as he spoke into the communications device.

Mogoma got no response to his distress signal. He looked down at the communication device and found that it was not transmitting or receiving any signals from himself or anyone in the Andromedan Imperial Army.

"Watch out, young Nommo. We might be on our own on this one," Mogoma whispered to Menzi. Menzi panted for desperate dread as he heard Mogoma's warning. He looked around and saw lobster-like creatures whose ill intentions were given away by their ghastly appearance.

Menzi and Mogoma were already exhausted from the epic battle they had with the Mathra armada when the Nommo were outside of the Mathra mothership. Menzi could hear thumping in his head as the Mathra around them hissed and growled and the Positive Logos started to cry.

"Stick close to me, young Nommo. Do not make direct contact with any of them. Whatever you do, make sure you stand your ground, do not panic, and do not by any means let go of the Positive Logos," Mogoma whispered to Menzi.

Menzi looked around at the menacing Mathra that surrounded them. The Mathra looked like anthropomorphic lobsters, with large, glowing eyes protruding at the top of their heads. They had exoskeletons and pincers at the end of their long arms.

They also had thick, bold antennae at the top of their heads that twitched left, right and in circles. They varied in height and size. Menzi could not tell how many Mathra were surrounding them, but he could not see past the crowd around him in any direction.

Menzi looked up and other than the occasional spark of lightning-like light, there was darkness. He did not know exactly where he was, but he could tell that he was in mid-air and that he was in a closed space that was at least as large as an open rugby field.

The Mathra began to slowly inch closer to them with a lack of urgency that betrayed their confidence that the Nommo could not escape. Mogoma adjusted his combat stance and allowed a blade to protrude out of this armour near his wrist.

The two Nommo warriors knew that the Mathra wanted to take the Positive Logos from them and give it to their leader, The Architect. Their leader would then combine the Positive Logos with the Negative Logos.

Once the Positive and Negative Logos were combined, The Architect would have infinite cosmic power over the universe. They understood that The Architect wanted to destroy all life in the universe and recreate the universe in his image, with himself as supreme ruler.

The Nommo warriors knew that they could not allow The Architect to get the Positive Logos as he already had the Negative Logos. They prepared themselves for battle, knowing that protecting the Positive Logos from the Mathra was a vital fight for life itself.

"Nommo warriors. I plead with you. Do not make this any more difficult for yourselves than it needs to be. Your resistance will be your undoing. You are being given the privilege to see the imminent lord of the cosmos before his moment. Choose wisely," said a voice from the crowd of Mathra carpenters.

"The Nommo have no direct quarrels with the Mathra. We are lovers of peace at our mother's request. But we cannot allow the Mathra to get the Logos. If it means that we must risk our lives to stop you from getting what you want, we are prepared to do just that," Mogoma retorted.

Menzi gulped, as it became clear to him just how high the stakes were at that very moment. The Positive Logos, which took the form of a human baby, started crying even louder and Menzi held it closer in a bid to comfort it into silence.

"No matter. You will miss out on our leader manifesting his destiny and we will have to pull the Positive Logos out of your cold dead hands," said the carpenter. The Mathra carpenters surrounding Menzi and Mogoma began to hiss in unison and the Nommo prepared themselves for the worst.

"ENOUGH!" shouted a shrill voice amongst the crowd of Mathra carpenters. The carpenters immediately fell silent and stopped moving. Some looked to each other, seemingly confused about what they had just heard.

Menzi and Mogoma, still standing back-to-back, turned around and looked at each other, confused. They noticed that in one section of the crowd surrounding them, the carpenters began to move and shift as if they were making way for someone to step out of the crowd and confront them.

Menzi could see glimmers of a green glow coming from one part of the crowd where the carpenters were quietly shifting. Some moved to the side and others bowed their heads down as they made way. A short figure made its way to the front of the crowd until it was in full view of Menzi and Mogoma.

Menzi looked at the new figure in shock and disgust. The figure was shorter than the carpenters with a different body structure. The figure was covered in an exoskeleton like the other Mathra.

The figure had insectoid eyes that had a menacing emptiness to them. It hissed as it walked up to Menzi and Mogoma. Menzi held the Positive Logos even closer to himself and inched even closer to Mogoma, who turned around until he was also facing the new figure.

"Mogoma, what is that? Is he The Architect?" Menzi whispered to the older, more experienced Nommo warrior.

"He is not The Architect," Mogoma responded, also whispering. "But he is one of The Architect's highest rank of servants. He is a Welder. They are the highest rank of Mathra servants and among the only ones that have ever been in the presence of The Architect," he added.

The figure gave Menzi a long look, almost as if he could read the young earth-raised Nommo's fear and anxiety. His gaze lingered on Menzi, staying cold and uninterrupted. Menzi tried to hide his nerves as he looked back at the Mathra creature.

The Welder made a noise that Menzi believed to be the equivalent of scoffing. The Welder turned to the Carpenters behind it. The Carpenters adjusted themselves as if to prepare for instructions from the Welder.

"Mathra servants, you have done well to recover the Positive Logos. Our mission is now accomplished. This planet serves no threat and no purpose to the Mathra now that the Positive Logos has been secured. I shall instruct the Masons to initiate warp travel so that the Architect can bond with the Positive Logos in the region of the Great Attractor," the Welder said.

"There will be none of that," Mogoma said calmly. The Welder's head sprang up as it heard the Nommo's voice object. The Welder turned around again, looking at Mogoma. The Nommo warrior stood still, unflinching in the face of possible defeat and certain danger.

The Welder Mathra paced towards Mogoma until it was standing in front of him and staring straight into his eyes. "And who is the lowly fish-man that hopes to stop us?" the Mathra asked as it exhaled a maniacal breath into Mogoma's face.

"You will not take the Positive Logos from us," Mogoma said with a devious, subtle smile on his face. "The Architect will never become the master of this or any other universe. The Mathra's war of retribution will fail. And if the Mathra continues to wage this war on life in the cosmos, they will all be destroyed," Mogoma said, unflinchingly.

The Welder first stared at Mogoma in silence. Moments after, the silence was broken by laughter from the Welder, which was followed slowly by a chorus of laughter from the surrounding Mathra Carpenters.

Menzi looked around as the laughs grew louder, tightening his grip on the Positive Logos. Out of the corner of his eye, Menzi could see Mogoma standing upright in front of the Welder, with no sign of fear that he would be harmed or defeated. Now sweating, Menzi only grew more confused.

"Whatever gambit you have to your chest that you are not letting us know about, Nommo warrior, your brother in arms certainly did not get the memo. He seems rather green around the gills, dare I say. He looks as nervous as you should be," the Welder remarked.

"You speak a great deal of war talk for someone who is supposedly so self-assured. If you are so sure that you have already won, why don't you just take the Positive Logos from us? As a matter of fact, why don't you just strike me down right now?" Mogoma challenged.

"Mogoma!" Menzi exclaimed, warning the Nommo warrior against further antagonising the Welder. Mogoma raised his hand at Menzi, signalling for him to remain quiet. Menzi stopped himself, wondering where Mogoma's seemingly misplaced confidence came from.

"If you would indulge me, Mathra, allow me an opportunity to talk you and your fellow foot soldiers off of the ledge," Mogoma offered. "Let's say you are able to take the Positive Logos away from my fellow Nommo and me. You take it to the Architect. That only means you will have the Andromedan army, the Nommo warriors and thousands of other nations on your heels, looking to defeat you and avoid their own demise. How does the Architect hope to stop them?"

The Welder responded with a brief indifferent shrug. "I don't busy myself with the business of thinking long-term, Nommo. I follow my orders and I get out of the way. Because I happen to believe in justice for those who chase it and I prefer my limbs intact," the Welder said with a cold stare.

Menzi, in earshot of the conversation between Mogoma and the Welder, gulped at the Mathra's remark. He held the Positive Logos until its head was lying on his shoulder, his eyes still scanning the dark room around him.

"Hey, little buddy!" Menzi said to the Positive Logos in a shaking voice struggling to feign optimism. "If you could do that thing where you destroyed the bad guys' spaceship with laser beams like you did the other day, now would be the perfect time to do just that," he whispered.

"Think about all of the life that you would wipe out and disrupt that had nothing to do with the oppression of the Mathra. The Andromedan Empire is a brutal colonial power, but the people of this very planet know nothing of the history of the Mathra and the Andromedans. Why destroy what is a wonderous universe for them over something they know nothing about?" Mogoma asked.

The Welder took one step back from Mogoma. The Welder looked around at the many Mathra Carpenters surrounding them and hissed. The other Mathra hissed along with the Welder as its attention turned back to Mogoma again.

"You really haven't been paying attention to what this is all about, have you?" the Welder asked, half laughingly. "I don't begrudge you that though. The Nommo have never been big fans of staying up to date with current affairs, have they?"

"That's fair," Mogoma conceded. "Did you know that there is a planet in the Sirius star system that gets one day of sustained daylight a year? Its positioning and distance from the two stars in the system means that it gets less light than the other planets around it. But on the day that it does get daylight, it is the brightest day anywhere in the Sirius system. It is, perhaps, the brightest day on any planet in the cosmos," the Nommo responded.

"And what's your point?" the Welder snarled.

"Even the darkest planets in the universe have things about them that are bright and beautiful. When you do away with this universe, you will be doing away with things that even you, as the Mathra, appreciate. There is another way to get justice for what was done to the Mathra at the hands of Andromeda. I'm not yet sure what that is, but you don't need to get in the way of your own escape," Mogoma suggested.

"You don't get it," the Welder said, dismissing Mogoma's reasoning. "You don't know what it's like to be displaced from the only home that you have ever known, just for that planet to be deconstructed to build a power station orbital ring around a star. You don't know what it's like to watch refuge ships with children in them get pelted to oblivion as they fail to navigate their way through asteroid belts. You don't know the feeling of having to seek refuge on the most uninhabitable planets, because you knew that your oppressors would not follow you to those planets. There is no beauty in this universe for the Mathra because all existence has ever been for us is hardship, suffering and strife. No number of pretty planets and stars will change that. We truly live in different universes. You live in a universe of tranquillity, peace, and wonder. We live in a universe of fear and oppression. Or maybe these are one universe, and your peace comes at the price of our oppression. You don't

38

get to tell us that this is a beautiful universe when our experience of it is so wildly different from yours. But whatever the reason, what you have known to be your only home will be wiped out and replaced with whatever it is that we see fit to take its place," the Welder said.

Mogoma smiled at the Welder. The Welder inched closer until the two were face-to-face. "And if we stop you...?" the Nommo asked.

"We would be more than happy to see you try your best, Nommo. But I think you will understand when I say that we as the Mathra would rather die than continue living the way Andromeda has forced us to," the Welder answered.

Clutching the Positive Logos in his arms, Menzi stared at the exchange while the Mathra Carpenters at the Welder's command continued staring at him. The Welder's attention then shifted to Menzi. "Now if you don't mind, we will be taking the Positive Logos now," the Welder said.

The Welder began walking towards Menzi with three sure steps before it stopped. Menzi gulped and closed his eyes, realising that he would have to engage the freakish alien creature in combat. He opened his eyes once again when he realised that its stride was halted.

He saw that Mogoma had grabbed the Welder's tail with his right hand. Menzi took a few steps back. The Welder turned around and gave Mogoma a cold stare. "You're not taking the Positive Logos unless and until you deal with me," Mogoma declared, still gripping the Welder's tail.

"You insolent vermin! I will destroy you and feed off your bones!" the Welder exclaimed. The Mathra took a swipe at Mogoma with its left claw, almost as if to swat at him like a bothersome fly. But the agile warrior, Mogoma, jumped eight feet into the air, evading the swipe.

Mogoma came back down with a spinning kick that whacked the Welder on the top of its head. The Welder stumbled for a step or two while Mogoma landed on two feet in a combative stance. Menzi stared at Mogoma, not knowing what to say or do.

"Get behind me, young Nommo," Mogoma advised, still in his combative stance and waiting for the Welder to come at him with a counterattack. Without a single word, Menzi scurried along with the Positive Logos still in his arms until he was standing behind Mogoma.

The Welder got back to its feet, a dark green substance now coming from its head where Mogoma had struck it. Its eyes glowed a vengeful and raging red. Mogoma did not let his gaze on the Welder break as he got back into his combative stance.

"You will regret the day that you did that, Nommo! Carpenters attack! And do not think of approaching my quarters unless it is to deliver the Positive Logos into my arms!" the enraged Welder said to the other Mathra.

Suddenly, Mogoma held his head and seethed in discomfort. This confused and scared Menzi. "Um, Mogoma? What's happening? Are you okay?" asked the young Nommo.

"I don't understand. Elder Amma...! I feel her life force extinguishing. Something is happening! She's...she's dying!" Mogoma strained. Menzi went numb at the news that the Elder of the planet Nibiru was no more.

The Carpenters let out croak-like sounds as they inched closer to Mogoma and Menzi. The Welder retreated into the crowd of Mathra Carpenters until it could not be seen by Menzi and Mogoma anymore.

"I don't mean to interrupt this for you, Mogoma, but we're in urgent trouble here," Menzi alerted Mogoma. One Mathra let out a primal growl as the others sprang forward to take Menzi and Mogoma down. Mogoma pulled out his traditional Nommo blade and began swiping at the Mathra Carpenters that were attacking him and Menzi.

More and more Mathra Carpenters sprang forward to attack the two Nommo warriors. Carrying the Positive Logos in his arms, Menzi's arms were not free for hand to hand combat and, perhaps more pertinent, he was too petrified by the scenes around him to put up a decent defence.

Menzi ducked to the ground until he and the Positive Logos were lying under Mogoma and between his legs. His view showed nothing but Mathra Carpenters and their legs as they pounced to attack Mogoma.

He could also hear Mogoma's yells and grunts as he fought the Mathra Carpenters off. Menzi wondered how the lone Nommo warrior was able to keep his cool in such a desperate situation, let alone defend both of them as well as the Positive Logos against such an onslaught.

He could hear the sounds of the Nommo blade striking the hard shells of the Mathra Carpenters' exoskeletons and their agonising growls as they hit the ground. Menzi was in awe of Mogoma's ability to hold his own in a battle so one-sided it should have been considered an ambush.

Menzi looked to the Positive Logos in his arms. The baby-like figure lay sleeping peacefully, but Menzi felt the temptation to wake the cosmic object up and use its infinite power to fight the Mathra Carpenters. Menzi desperately shook the Positive Logos to wake up.

"PLEASE HELP US!" Menzi cried out, as his screams were constantly getting engulfed by the din of battle around him. Suddenly, the Positive Logos opened its eyes, as they let out a blinding glow. Menzi immediately covered his eyes with his left hand, still carrying the Positive Logos in his right arm.

The glow from the Positive Logos' eyes continued, unrelenting. Menzi quickly realised that covering his eyes did not prevent the searing glow from penetrating

43

his vision. With his palm in front of his face, he still saw it. With his eyes closed, he still saw it.

He forced his eyes open and realised that the glow was engulfing him, the Positive Logos itself and Mogoma. It became so blinding that he could not see any of the Mathra foot soldiers that surrounded them just seconds ago.

He felt a force drift around him and realised immediately that he was somehow in motion. He looked down at the Positive Logos in his arms and saw it begin to vanish. He looked up and noticed that even Mogoma was starting to vanish.

"Oh, no! Oh, no, what's happening? What's going on?!" Menzi fretted. Menzi could no longer feel the ground beneath him as he suddenly shifted from laying on the ground to being in freefall in the middle of the blinding ether of light and silence.

Menzi could feel himself falling but could not make out anything near him that looked like solid ground. His balance and height perception could not even give him any sense of the direction in which he was falling.

As he continued to drift in the endless light, he heard a voice that he had never heard before but that had a familiar warmth to it. The voice said just eight words: "Remember Yasuke! Remember Queen Nzinga! Remember Mansa Musa!"

Suddenly, he felt himself move faster through the bright backdrop that surrounded him. He suddenly realised that he was no longer holding the Positive Logos in his arms. He looked in all directions around him, but he could not see Mogoma or the Positive Logos.

"Help! Please, someone, help me!" Menzi shouted. His screams were not heard by anyone. There was nothing around him but white light. He felt his body begin to warp as if the gravity of someplace would eventually catch him.

Menzi could feel his drifting gather pace and he began to see the colour around him begin to blur back into textures and shapes. His arms and legs flailed desperately as the environment around him slowly started to take shape.

Chapter 2: Sanctuary

Location: The Pleiadian sanctuary on the moon of Kappess

The Pleiadian monk, Tawa, was meditating in the sanctuary on the Kappess moon which he called his home his entire life. All of the Pleiadians were going about their usual business in their little corner of paradise.

As it has for millions of years, the world of the Pleiadians continued to avoid the chaos of the universe and its high stakes power struggles. If nothing else, it at least managed to maintain the appearance that it did.

The Pleiadian sanctuary was perpetually in a purple haze of tranquillity, with the backdrop always looking like a winter's sunset. Fountains flowed gently as the Pleiadian monks meditated, fetched water, farmed, and went about their day to day business.

The skies of the Kappess moon were never without a sun in the sky, as the moon was located in a densely packed part of space between the Milky Way and the Andromeda with thousands of stars of all sizes in the neighbourhood.

This civilisation was a direct antithesis of the Andromedan Empire, in that while Andromeda was ambitious, greedy and expansionist, the Pleiadians were nomadic-farmer conservationists, who did not consume more than they needed.

However, while the Pleiadians made a habit of keeping to themselves rather than building empires and subduing other civilisations, their ancient wisdom and incredible power made them an asset in the intergalactic geopolitical battles of the day.

Days ago, the Pleiadian Congress had a debate about whether the civilisation should involve itself in what was essentially a conflict between the Andromedans and the Mathra, even though the fate of the entire universe was at stake.

At the end of that meeting, it was the leader of the Pleiadians, Mogori, who had his way. He submitted that the Pleiadians should remain involved in the conflict and remain on the side of the Andromedan Empire.

Tawa differed with Mogori and was of the view that the oppressive and avaricious Andromedan Empire was not worthy of Pleiadian allegiance. Tawa could not, however, present a viable alternative to stopping the Mathra's plan if the Pleiadians withdrew their support of Andromeda.

Tawa sat at the top of a small hill in a meditative state, levitating and letting off a bright blue glow. Other Pleiadians farmed, chanted, and joined in meditations. The highest star in the sky was a distant blue giant while others were on the other end of the Kappess moon, giving the sky a purple hue.

Tawa suddenly opened his eyes as he could sense an energy that he could not explain was nearby. He looked around and noticed that the other Pleiadians also raised their heads, betraying their awareness of the shift in the environment as well.

Mogori emerged from the sanctuary's temple. He was the leader and elder of the Pleiadians, playing a role in the Pleiades that was not too different from the role that Elder Amma played among the Nommo on planet Nibiru.

As Mogori walked out of the temple, the other Pleiadians stood up and turned in his direction in acknowledgement. Mogori slowly walked out into the sanctuary looking around himself. The sanctuary fell silent.

Mogori moved towards the open field space where congress meetings took place. He stopped at the smooth patch of ground he usually sat at during meetings, but he did not immediately sit down. The other Pleiadians stared at him.

"Does anybody else feel that? An energy is amongst us that was not here before. It's somewhat familiar, but alien. It...it doesn't feel like a threat or an attack. But it is certainly not of Pleiadian origin," Mogori observed.

"Yes. Yes, we all feel it," Tawa responded. "But our watchers would have given us a signal if any visitors came to Kappess, Father. Unless, of course, they travelled here through other means. Speaking of travelling, do we have any word from Taheeq in the Milky Way galaxy?" Tawa asked.

"Yes," Mogori replied. "Taheeq told me that two Nommo warriors were captured by the Mathra with the Positive Logos in their possession. There is no indication of what has happened since, but Taheeq is asking us to prepare for the possibility that The Architect has already combined it with the Negative Logos," he added grimly.

"Something tells me that if The Architect had the Positive Logos in his hands, he would not waste any time. He would have already started unravelling the very fabric of the universe. And as far as I can tell, nothing is particularly different," Tawa suggested optimistically.

"You have a point. But that doesn't mean that we can afford to breathe a sigh of relief. We need to plan what we do next and act. The Nommo are good friends of ours and we must help them at this time," Mogori said as he walked past some of the Pleiadians prostrating themselves before him.

The Pleiadians began to murmur and whisper amongst themselves. The news that the Mathra had gotten closer than ever before to seizing the Positive Logos stoked speculation of how much time they, and the entire universe, really had.

"Personally, even though we have decided to align ourselves with the Andromedan Empire, I think it would be prudent of us to reassess our plan of action as the Pleiadians. At least where it relates to the Positive and Negative Logos," Tawa said.

The murmurs from the other Pleiadians stopped after Tawa spoke. They all turned to Tawa, as if to search him for an explanation. Mogori turned to Tawa and tilted his head. "And what exactly do you mean by that, Tawa?" he asked.

All eyes were now on Tawa. He looked around at his brothers in the sanctuary and then he turned to his spiritual father, Mogori, whose gaze had not shifted from the Pleiadian since he uttered his suggestion. Tawa sighed and raised his hands decorously.

"Okay, fine. I am just going to come out and say it. I think we need to ditch the plan of the Andromedan Empire and work to keep the Positive and Negative Logos for ourselves. Then we can use them as we see fit," Tawa blurted out.

The Pleiadians started to mutter amongst themselves in hysterics as soon as they heard Tawa's suggestion. Mogori smiled to himself as he heard Tawa's suggestion. He walked back to his patch on the field and sat down, positioning himself so that he was still facing Tawa, who was standing on a hill.

"Tawa, you know the ways we have pledged to honour. We are not about shaping the universe in one way or the other. We are not like Andromeda or the Mathra. That's simply not something that the Pleiadians do," Mogori retorted.

"And maybe that's the problem! Maybe that is the reason why, even though we live with plenty and abundance, we find ourselves in a universe that is steeped in destruction, oppression, hunger, and doom. We know how to overcome these things. We must share," said Tawa.

"Oh, come on, Tawa!" Mogori admonished. "Can you even hear what you sound like right now? You sound exactly like the Andromedan propagandists who go on and on about how their colonial ways 'civilised' so-called lesser people!" he said.

"We will do things differently, father. I know we will! If the Logos has the power to destroy the entire universe down to the last atom, then it has creative power as well. We can use that power to increase resources. We will rebuild every planet that the Andromedans stripped down for power swarm stations. We could replenish every natural resource that Andromeda has depleted for a day's energy. We can even restore the lives that were taken during their campaign to establish their oppressive colonies. Make more room! We can create a universe where there is no pollution and there is food, protection, and shelter for everyone. We live it right now, but we have an opportunity to create a paradise for trillions of other souls in this cold and lonely universe." Tawa said.

"Look. I know it sounds like it's the right thing in your head. But interfering in how the universe works is not wise. Even with the best of intentions. Our mission should remain the same. The addition of more resources to the universe will only invite more growth and more demands of the fundamentally finite resources," Mogori warned.

"Then on top of adding resources to the universe, we enlighten the civilisations of the universe. We teach them how we managed to keep ourselves alive while keeping our own resources abundant. We enlighten them to our way of life. That's what we do with the Logos!" Tawa said, his pitch rising.

"That's exactly how we ended up in this situation in the first place, don't you see?" Mogori pushed back. "Thinking we can make decisions for other peoples. Imposing our way on them, thinking that our ways are inherently superior. Do you honestly think the Andromedan Empire set out to make the universe worse?" he insisted.

Tawa fell silent, realising that he would not win the elder over in the argument. He looked around. The other Pleiadians looked in his direction, but none would look him in the eye. He turned back to Mogori and shrugged half-heartedly.

"So, no hope? We defeat the Mathra and make no use of the Logos in any way. And then everyone goes back to where they came from, no matter how much or how little they had before the fact? Back to an unequal, unjust universe?" Tawa asked rhetorically.

"We don't choose the situations that we find ourselves in, Tawa! But I, for one, will not stand by and watch my people play God with the ways of the universe, regardless of how well-intentioned it might be!" Mogori said as a tear streamed down his face.

The Pleiadians were stunned to silence yet again, not used to seeing their elder lose his temper or get emotional to the point of shedding tears. They looked on at their stoic leader with confusion and sadness.

Tawa's eyes also started to fill up with tears. Debates between the Pleiadians were always honest and blunt, but never before had an argument between the Pleiadians in the Kappess sanctuary become as emotionally charged as this one had.

Tawa raised his hands again, indicating that he had no desire to drag the quarrel out any further. Mogori let out a dejected sigh. Tawa turned his back to the other Pleiadians as the tears started to stream down his face.

Suddenly, the faint sounds of crying could be heard in the sanctuary. The Pleiadians looked up and around, noticing the sound, but unaware of where it was coming from. Tawa moved away from the other Pleiadians and looked around him, trying to locate the source of the sound.

Mogori stood up, also noticing the sound of faint crying in the sanctuary. Tawa walked towards some bushes, the sound getting clearer the more he headed in that direction, although the sound was not particularly loud at all.

"That is very odd. All the children are sleeping at the nursery. Why would a child be left here amongst us while we discuss matters of congress?" Mogori asked himself. The other Pleiadians also looked around, trying to locate the source of the sound.

"It's not any of our children, that's for sure. It sounds...different, somehow. I wonder if it has anything to do with that new presence that we just felt. What do you think, father?" Tawa asked Mogori.

"You're right," Mogori answered, now right behind Tawa. "It sounds different from any of our children or any lifeform that exists here on Kappess. Whatever it is, it is in those bushes and its presence is remarkably powerful," he added.

Tawa slowly approached a bush that had a glow emanating from it. He carefully cleared some sticks and stems from obscuring his view of what was waiting behind the bush. To Tawa's surprise, he saw a lone baby lying in the bush, glowing and crying.

The group of Pleiadians behind the two gasped and whispered, astonished by what they were seeing. Tawa stared, mesmerised while Mogori looked on with no reaction. The baby was still glowing and crying, although it showed no sign of being injured or in distress.

"Is that...the Positive Logos...?" Tawa asked.

"Yes. Yes, it is. This answers some important questions for us, Tawa," said Mogori. "It appears that the Positive Logos saved itself from the clutches of the Mathra by teleporting itself to our sanctuary," he said.

"It has indeed," said Tawa, still looking at the baby's mesmerising glow. "And regardless of what it is that we decide to do, the Positive Logos has seemingly blessed us with an opportunity to save the universe…"

Chapter 3: Lost In The Cosmos

Location: The cosmic brain, somewhere in the universe

Menzi opened his eyes and saw amber lights shimmering in a fluid blur. He gasped and immediately started to fidget frantically as soon as he realised that water started flowing down his throat when he drew a breath in.

What would have been screams were panicked muffles from his mouth. He saw more and more bubbles emerging rising above him, realising that they were escaping from his mouth. Swimming was not a challenge for Menzi, but the sudden realisation that he was underwater caught him off guard.

His movements steadied as he realised that he was in the water. He adjusted himself until he was floating vertically. Menzi looked around him and noticed that he was in an enormous body of water, but that it did not have the typical blue hue of water from the seas and oceans on earth.

The water he was in had no chill or coolness to it. He felt it easier to float in this water. He looked down to the bed of the body of water he was in and saw strange aquatic life in the depths that he did not recognise from any biology textbook.

Menzi looked back up and saw the visage of a purple sky with a few red spots of light in the sky. He started to swim upwards to get to the surface of the water. His head emerged at the surface and Menzi began to cough violently, spewing out the water that filled his throat moments ago.

Menzi looked around but he could not see any dry land anywhere around him. The surface of the water had a dark purple look to it, reflecting the colour of the sky. He looked up and saw two red lights in the sky, flickering on and off slowly.

"Where am I...?" he panted to himself as he looked around confused. "Oh, my God. The baby! Where is the baby?" he exclaimed. Menzi started bobbing his head under the water, hoping he could locate the Positive Logos and recover it.

Just moments ago, Menzi recalled having the Positive Logos in his arms, while Mogoma was preparing to fend off a mob of Mathra foot soldiers. The next moment he recalled being surrounded by light after the Positive Logos started glowing mysteriously.

Suddenly he found himself in an unfamiliar location in the water. He could tell by the location's appearance that he was most likely not on planet Earth anymore. He continued floating at the surface looking around him for the Positive Logos.

Menzi floated in the softly drifting waters helplessly. He sulked as his panting slowed down, with tears brimming at the corner of his eyes. At a loss for what he should do next, Menzi tried to get his bearings straight.

He looked up and saw a distant white figure flying in the sky. The figure left a trail of light that faded moments later. Menzi managed to get a closer look at the figure, thanks to his Nommo abilities. He saw that the figure was a humanoid figure riding on what appeared to be a wakeboard attached to a large sail.

Menzi figured that whatever was riding this flying this board was headed somewhere with dry land and resources, he started trailing behind the figure. The young Nommo immediately noticed how fast and easily he moved through the water as he swam.

As a Nommo, Menzi had strength, speed, and stamina beyond that of any human. This allowed him to keep up with the flying vehicle. The wakeboard-like vehicle stopped moving and stayed still in the air for a moment. Menzi stopped swimming so that he was floating in the water right beneath it.

Menzi looked up, wondering why the vehicle had stopped moving. Suddenly it started to descend until it was just above the water. Menzi backstroked to make room for the vehicle as well as create enough room for him to escape if he needed to.

Menzi looked and realised that the individual on the board was robotic in appearance. It looked humanoid but was genderless in appearance. Its body was grey in colour, and it seemed smooth at its joints and contours. It had a hollow space with a red light beaming out where its face would have been.

The humanoid machine's board stopped descending when it was floating just above the water. It turned its head in Menzi's direction. Menzi gulped as he floated just a few feet away from the machine, ready to explain himself or run.

The machine adjusted itself until it was sitting on the board with its legs dangling over, still facing Menzi. The two stared at each other in silence. The board floated closer to Menzi. The Nommo gasped anxiously but did not attempt to maintain the distance.

The machine's head tilted as it started making incomprehensible noises. Menzi looked back at a loss for words. The machine's grinding and hissing noises started up again. Suddenly the light emanating from its head projected on Menzi's face as the machine went silent.

"Green scaly skin. A fin on the cranium. Large, aquatic eyes. Yes. Yes, you are most certainly a Nommo," the humanoid machine said as it assessed Menzi. "You have chosen a very interesting place to hide yourself."

"Yes, well, I'm sorry. I don't know. I don't know..." Menzi stammered as he tried to respond. "I'm sorry. I didn't mean to trespass into your home. I don't know where I am and I don't know how I got here," Menzi responded.

"Evidently, yes," the machine responded. "But not to worry. I have a suspicion that I know exactly why you are here. In fact, for the longest time, we, the Zeta Reticuli at the cosmic brain have been expecting you," it said.

"You've been expecting me? Did you bring me here? If so, I'm going to need you to take me back to where I was. I was in the middle of something really important and the fate of the universe might be at stake," Menzi fumbled.

"Yes, I'm afraid it's not that simple. We did not send you here. But we were advised very long ago by your elder that we should expect one of you to visit us. And if that is why you were sent here, then you are exactly where you need to be at the moment," the humanoid responded.

"Wait. You've been expecting me? How is that possible? Who are you? And where am I?" Menzi asked.

"I am Sheh. I am one of the Zeta Reticuli. You are in the orbit of a cosmic brain in the outskirts of the cosmos," the humanoid machine said.

"Cosmic brain? Zeta Retic-what!" Menzi repeated.

"You do not know about our civilisation?" the Zeta Reticuli observed.

"Sorry if I'm supposed to. I didn't grow up on Nibiru like other Nommo. I'm from a planet called Earth in a galaxy called the Milky Way. It's one of the galaxies that's close to Andromeda. Do you know the

Andromedan Empire? They have scary, mean orange ladies," Menzi explained.

"I know the galaxy you're talking about. And the planet," Sheh responded lightly. "We passed by there a long way back. How are those giant lizards doing?" Sheh asked.

"The dinosaurs? They're all gone. They've been dead for over sixty million years," Menzi said.

"Oh, well. No surprises there," Sheh huffed. Sheh adjusted themselves until their machine body was standing on the board again. They extended their hand to Menzi. "Come up. I'll take you somewhere you can dry up," Sheh offered.

Menzi stretched out his hand as Sheh pulled him up out of the water and onto the board. Sheh grabbed a beam that anchored the now collapsed sail of the vehicle they had been travelling on. Sheh invited Menzi to stand behind them and hold onto their shoulders.

The board levitated higher until it was some forty feet above the water. The sail unfurled and took shape in the wind. The board began moving immediately. Menzi enjoyed the rush of wind in his hair as the board glided along. The atmosphere dazzled Menzi with colours he had never seen before.

"So, Sheh. I see you're a machine of some sort. Are you someone's helper? Is your civilisation run by machines? And what was it that brought you to our planet?" Menzi gushed.

"I am not a machine. I am a sentient consciousness that uploaded itself to a machine body. Myself and other Zeta Reticuli like me live in a device called the cosmic brain. Our consciousnesses were uploaded to it, but occasionally we use robot bodies, like this one, as avatars to move around in this universe," Sheh explained.

"Woah. So, your entire civilisation uploaded their souls to a giant computer? So does that mean you live in a simulation?" Menzi inquired.

"Yes. We found a way to preserve our consciousness beyond what mortal years would allow. Our simulation affords us all the resources we need without taking from anyone else or wasting existing resources. All we need is energy from the accretion disk around a black hole to keep the cosmic brain running," Sheh explained.

"Wow. This really sounds like something out of a sci-fi movie. Why did you do it? Why did you decide to live in a simulation?" Menzi asked.

"We decided at a time when the universe was hostile and short on resources. We travelled the universe and saw much of all there was to see. It's a hard place to exist in. We decided to create a simulated world that would upload our collective consciousness. Freed from the prison of our physical bodies, we freed ourselves from the need for food, shelter, and the need to classify ourselves by race, class, or gender. We also created avatars, like the one you see before you now, to access this physical universe. We mostly do this to maintain and do repairs on the cosmic brain and make sure that there are no intruders in the neighbourhood. The cosmic brain alerted us to a new presence, so I plugged my consciousness into this robot body to check things out, and here you are," Sheh said.

Menzi's mouth gaped open as Sheh spoke. He shook his head briefly. "This is fascinating! Just the whole idea of a civilisation creating a simulation and uploading themselves to it. It would sound horrifying where I'm from, but you sound content. And to traverse the whole universe, only to decide that there's nothing special about it and retreat into a simulation?

My people are definitely not mature enough to do that!" Menzi marvelled.

"The universe is a young place with many young civilisations. The Nommo are an ancient civilisation on any civilisation's standards, but the civilisation that you lived in is likely still in its infancy if they emerged after the giant lizards," Sheh explained.

"So, do you know the Nommo well? I only found out that I was a Nommo just the other day, so I can't exactly say that I know them very well. Sad, isn't it? I don't even know my people. And the people I do identify with are quite pathetic compared to the civilisations I've encountered lately," Menzi said.

"I wouldn't worry too much if I were you," Sheh said.

"I don't even know how to use my Nommo abilities!" Menzi moaned. "The Nommo I have met are these strong, courageous warriors and I can't even fight as they do. I lost the Positive Logos in the middle of a fight with the Mathra, while I ran and hid," he lamented.

"It sounds like you've been through a lot in a remarkably short space of time, young Nommo. It's hard to be a hero when it was not a life you were prepared for years ahead of time. I know Elder Amma would be very proud of you. As for the Positive Logos, the fact that the universe still appears intact is a sign that it hasn't fallen into the hands of the Mathra yet," Sheh explained.

"I never got to meet Elder Amma. Have you ever met her? Mogoma described her to me. Forgive me if this sounds a little on the nose, but from what I've heard she sounds like something out of this world," Menzi said.

"She talked to us about a lot of things. She entrusted a plan to us to stop the Mathra from destroying the universe. We spoke about it quite recently. Pretty much as soon as the Mathra revolt began," Sheh said.

"Wait a second. If you're having meetings with Elder Amma to stop the Mathra, then why didn't you come to earth with the Andromedan army to fight the Mathra head-on with us?" Menzi interrogated.

"For starters, we did not want to get involved in the campaign with the Andromedans or the geopolitical battles of this universe. And secondly, we just did this as a favour for Elder Amma," Sheh replied.

Menzi frowned as he considered Sheh's answer. The board ascended higher into the sky until Menzi could make out where he was from a distance. The edge of the structure that the water was on appeared rugged and asymmetrical and Menzi could tell that it was a stationary asteroid.

The board began to approach a large, moon-like structure with a massive tunnel at its centre. It was the cosmic brain. It had a large red light slowly flickering at its centre from the depths of the tunnel. Menzi gawked, looking around as they entered the tunnel.

The board settled in a room that had a smaller passage in it. Sheh hopped off. Menzi followed Sheh as the Zeta Reticuli walked towards the passage. Sheh stood in front of a white wall with an insignia engraved on it.

The light in Sheh's head projected onto the insignia and the wall opened up to reveal a closet-like compartment with a couple of items inside. At the same time a platform rose from the ground to serve as a table or counter. Sheh took the items in the compartment and placed them on the platform.

"The truth is, Elder Amma was counting on coming back here. But we haven't seen her yet. But what she wanted to come here and do is something only a Nommo can do. How familiar are you or the civilisation of earth with traversing the timespan?" Sheh asked.

"Time travel? Seriously...?" Menzi asked as he hooded his eyes.

"Yes, but not quite," Sheh corrected. "The Nommo are all connected through the ties of artifacts and items that belong to them. Elder Amma used this ability to go to different times in the history of the earth and leave different fragments of a weapon there with those she trusted. The plan was for her to come back, go back to those periods and retrieve the weapon from those she entrusted it with. It's something she planned to do, but really, any Nommo can do it," they added.

Menzi rubbed his temples as his eyes shut tight. "Wait. You're asking me to go back in time to the past on my home planet and look for weapons? Wait. That must have been what that voice I heard before I was transported here meant."

"What voice?" Sheh asked.

"As I was being taken away from the Mathra ship, I heard a voice saying something. It said...um...it said: 'Remember Yasuke, remember Queen Nzinga and remember Mansa Musa'. Yes. That's it, I remember," Menzi recalled roughly.

Sheh paused. "Menzi, if that was the voice of Elder Amma, then there is a good chance that something happened to her," they said ominously.

"What?" Menzi asked. Sheh moved around the platform until they were right in front of Menzi and grabbed his shoulders firmly.

"This means that it has to be you that goes on this mission and there is no time to waste. You will have to go to the people she mentioned in the message she sent you and recover fragments of the weapon from them," Sheh said.

"But how? I don't know how to travel in time!" Menzi protested.

"Everything that you need to complete the mission is here. And the mission will have to be completed by you. Because young Nommo, I don't want to sound like I'm exaggerating here, but the fate of the universe still rests on your shoulders right now. Perhaps now more than ever before," Sheh said.

Menzi gulped momentarily but then a frown took hold of his face. "She me what I need to do and I will do it," he said.

Sheh took a katana from the platform and a silver-coloured, sage-like herb. He took the items and placed them on the floor in front of Menzi. Sheh went down on their knees and motioned Menzi to do the same.

Menzi went down on his knees so that he was facing Sheh directly. He looked at the sage-like herb and recognised it, not just for its resemblance to normal sage on earth, but because it its resemblance to a tool Mogoma taught him to use to communicate with his earthly brother Nathi.

"I take it you're familiar with this," Sheh said holding up the herb. "This will be what you use to travel back. This item belonged to the first person that you are going to meet. They will give you the first artefact you need as well as an item you need to find the next person. The second person will have an artefact as well as a third item which will lead you to a third person. They will give you the third and final piece to the puzzle of a powerful weapon. If you are still alive by the end of the mission, Elder Amma indicated that you should be able to make your way back to where you belong with no problem. This weapon is not as powerful as the Positive Logos when combined with the Negative Logos, but it should give you a fighting chance," Sheh explained.

Menzi nodded. He grabbed the herb and used a laser from his armour's wristband to set it on fire. He put the herb on the floor and allowed it to burn until its smoke rose. He placed the katana right above the smoke as it smouldered.

"Elder Amma. I call to you as a son of the Nommo. I ask you to guide me as I travel. Spirit of the Nommo, I plead with you to guide me. Be my eyes. Be my intuition. Light my path and guide my way," Menzi shouted.

Small sparks developed in the smoke from the burning herb. Menzi opened his eyes as he heard the sound of rumbling. The sparks increased in frequency and a pathway formed in front of Menzi and Sheh.

Menzi stood back up, with the katana in hand. He turned to Sheh. "I can't join you on this journey. Only a Nommo can go through that passage. And it is your journey to see through young Nommo. I wish you the best of luck," they said.

Menzi nodded. He turned to the portal and began to step into it, with the katana in one hand and the herb in the other.

"And Menzi," Sheh called out. Menzi turned to Sheh again. "You can do it. And honestly, you're going to have to be able to do it. Because if you don't do it, the universe might just be out of luck," Sheh said bluntly.

Menzi looked into the portal. Sparks crackled like tiny bolts of lightning as Menzi stepped into the portal to go into a familiar world at a long-gone time.

Chapter 4: To The Pleiades

Location: Planet Earth in the Milky Way galaxy

Pandemonium got hold of the Mathra Carpenters in the section of the mothership where Menzi, Mogoma and the Positive Logos had been cornered without any chance of escape just moments ago. The alien foot soldiers scrambled amongst themselves to make sense of what had just happened.

The Carpenters panicked, looking around the vessel for the two Nommo warriors and the Positive Logos that had just vanished before their eyes. They made crackling sounds similar to that of cockroaches as they scrambled frantically.

"Where is the Positive Logos," hissed the Welder that gave the Carpenters their orders. "If we return to the Architect empty-handed, he will have all of us put to death, including me! So, you had better find the Positive Logos and find it immediately," the Welder raged.

"They were right here just a moment ago," said a Carpenter as he looked behind a wall. "But it seems that they have disappeared without a trace. It seems

75

that they are not here anymore," the Carpenter
continued.

"Well, thank you for the insightful and novel
observation, Captain Obvious!" the Welder snapped.
"We have to find them. Find the Positive Logos! We
are too close to realising our mission to be denied
now!" he exclaimed to the entire room.

"Welder," said a voice amongst the crowd of Mathra
foot soldiers. "I swear, if you are calling me to make
another idiotic, counterproductive observation, I will
tell the Architect myself that he ought to put you to
death first!" the Welder snapped.

"No Welder. The steps in the hallway are getting
louder. It's a Sculptor," the Carpenter corrected. "A
Sculptor is on their way here. And they are bringing
The Architect with them," the Carpenter said grimly.

The Welder froze. The room of panicking Mathra
Carpenters suddenly fell quiet. The footsteps down the
hall got loud enough for all the Mathra in the
container room to hear. They heard three sets of
footsteps, with one sounding distinctly different from
the other two.

The two sets of footsteps that had a deep vibration with each step were the footsteps of two Mathra Sculptors. The third set of footsteps, which was lighter in sound and had a swish to them, were those of the Architect.

Three shadows bled onto the floor near the entrance of the container room and grew taller and taller. The Carpenters arranged themselves to prostrate before their ruler. Accepting that there was nothing else he could do, the Welder walked towards the door, ready to tell the Architect the bad news.

The Sculptors appeared at the doorway, side by side. They had long, slender bodies, in a silver exoskeleton. Their large heads resembled those of praying mantis but also had a silver colour to them. They carried sceptres and had long necks as well as long legs.

"Mathra servants, bow to your knees, quiet your voices, and prepare to receive your king and the king of the cosmos. He is here. The lord of all creation. The Architect," said one of the Sculptors.

The Sculptors stood to the side to make way for the Architect. The now silent Carpenters took to their knees and fixed their foreheads on the floor, as if too terrified to look the Architect in the face once he entered the room.

The Architect stood at the entrance of the container room, slightly behind the Sculptors who had just introduced him. His visage made a shadowy figure whose eyes still pierced menacingly into the room as they glowed a deep red. A red glow also came from the left side Architect's abdomen.

The Architect came into full view as he walked into the container room. Even for creatures as alien as the Mathra, the Architect looked wildly different from his subordinates and was even more horrifying in his appearance than the rest of them.

The Architect had multiple shades and textures of dull green, some with an exoskeleton sheen and others resembling reptilian scales. The Architect was shorter than the Mathra of lower rank. He had a squatty, broad body with skinny, fragile-looking limbs that twitched uncontrollably.

His face had wrinkling skin that resembled worn leather while his eyes were completely pitch black with no sign of feeling, compassion, or life. From the left side of his abdomen hung a glowing red, tumour-like object that seemed to attach itself to him with appendages.

The Architect shuffled until he was in front of the Welder, as the army of Carpenters and the two Sculptors surrounded them. The Welder stood in front of the Architect facing the ground for the shame of his failure. The Architect opened his mouth to speak but coughed before he started.

"Welder. You promised your master that you would do right by the Mathra on this day. Do not let this be another moment where you have disappointed me," the Architect said staring the Welder in the face.

"Master. I...I had the Positive Logos right here. It was in our sights, and we had accomplished the mission," the Welder stammered. "The Nommo pulled another one of their dirty tricks and now they and the Positive Logos have disappeared," he explained.

"Welder. You have failed me yet again. Not only have you failed to bring me closer to becoming lord of the universe, the consequences of your continued failure to retrieve the Positive Logos grow more dire for your master with every passing day," the Architect said.

The Welder took a step back and looked at the Architect in the face. "Master, how? I don't understand what you are saying," the Welder fumbled.

The Architect began to nurse the glowing object on his side as he winced in pain. The object started glowing brighter. The Architect gnashed and coughed before continuing to explain to the Welder.

"The Negative Logos," he said, still touching the object. "It is feeding off of my life force and will not stop until it is depleted. I have time, but only so much. The negative energy in the Negative Logos has been poisoning me every day since it was surgically bonded with me. So, you see, Welder, your incompetence is more than just an inconvenience to me. It threatens to end my life," the Architect seethed.

The Welder went down on one knee. The position placed him closer to the Negative Logos in the Architect's body. The vantage point allowed him to see what looked like a grotesque face trapped in the Architect's abdomen, writhing in pain.

"It won't happen again, Master," the Welder stammered again. "Give me another chance. I will set course for the planet and find those two Nommo parasites. I will recover the Positive Logos and return with their decapitated heads on a platter for you, my lord," the Welder pleaded.

"It's too late, Welder. You have disappointed your master for the last time. I will find the Positive Logos without you, and you will be denied the privilege of seeing your lord become the master of the cosmos. Come forward and accept your punishment," the Architect said flatly.

Mathra Carpenters in the room fought the urge to gasp. The Welder took two steps back, devastated by what he had just heard the Architect say. After a moment of trembling, the Welder stepped forward, in acceptance that there was nothing that he could do to save himself.

He stepped forward until he was standing right before the Architect and then turned his back. The Welder raised his hands, fell to his feet, and closed his eyes. Slight whimpers of fear hopped around the container

81

room as the Carpenters, still bowing, waited to see what would happen next.

The Architect raised his hands as he stood behind the Carpenter. The Negative Logos attached to the Architect's side glowed brighter as the Architect groaned. Red glowing tentacles emerged from the Negative Logos still attached to the Architect's body.

The tentacles grew longer and longer. They suddenly sprang forward to the Welder's back, entering the foot soldier's body. The Welder briefly winced in agony as the tentacles violently undulated inside of his body.

The force of the tentacles shook the Welder's body, pulling it this way and pushing it that way. The Welder's eyes rolled over as he mustered up one more pitiful groan. Suddenly the tentacles ripped their way out of the Welder's body with the Welder's entrails in their grip.

The Welder's body fell forward until it was lying on its stomach. The Welder's back was ripped open with the innards of the Welder's body visibly dismembered. Some of the Carpenters could not help but gasp in horror at what they had just witnessed.

"Let that be a warning to everyone. Your lord will not tolerate incompetence. Not this close to the end of our mission. This Negative Logos might be draining my life force, but my physical attachment to it has given me the power to make your lives most miserable if you fail me," the Architect warned.

The Architect turned around and walked out of the room. The two accompanying Sculptors accompanied him. The Mathra Carpenters remained dead quiet long after the Architect had left the room.

"Sculptor, inform the Masons and the Welders that we are going to leave the orbit of this planet and pursue the Positive Logos. We will warp to the area of its new location," the Architect asked one of the Sculptors as he coughed.

"Master, we do not have pinpoint coordinates, but all indications are that the energy signature of the Positive Logos is no longer on this planet or in this star system," said one of the Sculptors walking with him.

"Thanks, but I already know that, genius," The Architect stopped the Sculptor, as he looked down at the glowing Negative Logos on his abdomen. "The Negative Logos senses where the Positive Logos is in the universe. It's not an exact science, but it's something," the Architect explained.

The Sculptors looked back at their master stunned. They were not sure about whether they should offer up the destination to protect themselves from their autocratic leader's wrath. "So where is it? Where are we going?" one Sculptor asked.

"For some reason, the Positive Logos saw it fit to teleport itself to one of the most peaceful sanctuaries in the universe. So, we will follow it there. To Kappess moon. Set coordinates for the ship to head to the Pleiades," the Architect said.

Meanwhile in Durban, Earth.

"What do you mean you don't know where the Nommo boy and the Positive Logos are?!" shouted an incredulous Princess Innozia.

The soldiers at her command watched Andromedan princess as she punched a hole in the ground from sheer frustration. They were no longer in combat with the Mathra, but the mission to stop the Mathra from getting the Positive Logos was still very much in the balance.

The Mathra ship hovered above the planet ominously as the soldiers of the Andromedan army on earth regrouped to strategise. Taheeq the Pleiadian stood in a corner by himself, eyes glowing blue and in a trance.

"We were fighting off the Mathra and suddenly the Positive Logos started acting out and teleported the three of us. I don't know where Kwataar (*Menzi's Nommo name) and the Positive Logos went, but the next thing I knew, when the blinding lights were gone, I was here with you," said Mogoma.

"Well, frankly, that doesn't cut it as an explanation, and it does not tell us where the Positive Logos is! If we can't recover it and keep it from the Mathra this whole mission could be rendered a failure. I mean, what if the Mathra have already used it?" Innozia lamented.

"I think if the Mathra had already used the Logos, we would have noticed a change in the environment around us. But so far, nothing is different. That must mean that they haven't gotten the Positive Logos yet," said Mogoma optimistically.

"You'd better be right, Nommo. In any event, I believe we should head straight to the Mathra ship and bring the war straight to them. A sheer show of force to let them know that we are not backing down," Innozia said.

"Princess Innozia," Taheeq said. "I have just heard from my brothers in the Kappess sanctuary that the Positive Logos is with them," Taheeq said loudly. Innozia turned to Taheeq, stunned by the sudden development.

The Mathra ship in the sky gave off a powerful vibration that caused everyone to look up at it. As the Andromedan soldiers looked at the Mathra ship, it began to shimmer until it had disappeared altogether. Innozia looked up stunned at how fast the mission had just further complicated itself.

Chapter 5: The Work of a Hero

Location: Feudal Japan

Year: circa 1582

Menzi emerged from the cloudy portal looking around him. As he walked out into an open field in Japan, he recalled the mysterious voice that he heard in the Mathra ship before the Positive Logos teleported him out of harm's way.

"Remember Yasuke! Remember Queen Nzinga! Remember Mansa Musa!" Menzi struggled with the meaning of these words. He knew the names mentioned in the message, but he could not figure out why they were relevant to his mission. Was it a riddle? Was it a prayer?

He chewed on a special herb grown on planet Nibiru, which empowered the Nommo with the ability to understand and speak the language of whoever it was that they were conversing with. He saw the landscape of the Tenmoku mountain adorned with lush forest trees and majestic peaks.

Menzi strode out, captivated by the beauty of the landscape he just walked into. But moments after he looked around and slowed down. He noticed a pillar of smoke rising from the distance. When his eyes followed the column of smoke to a castle that had just been set on fire.

Not far from him, two groups were on opposite ends of a field having a stare down. He looked at the battle armours of the people in the crowds and the architecture around him and concluded that he was likely in Japan.

And then it hit him. Was the voice he heard when he was teleported away from the Mathra the voice of Elder Amma? If this was indeed Japan, did Elder Amma send Menzi here to find the legendary black samurai Yasuke?

Menzi looked at one of the crowds, secretly relieved that all he would need to do to find Yasuke was find an African man in samurai regalia. And at that moment, he saw what he was looking for. A tall African man stood next to a Japanese commander.

Other than being the only dark skinned person there, besides Menzi, Yasuke was the tallest man on the battlefield. The samurai looked strong and regal. The historical accounts did not do justice to the towering figure he cut amongst other formidable warriors.

Menzi stayed among the tall trees, away from the sight of either of the camps. The commander leading Yasuke into battle was likely his mentor, the mighty daimyo Oda Nobunaga. Menzi remembered reading about Yasuke's life at his high school library.

He remembered reading about how Yasuke travelled to Japan from an unknown origin in Africa and was adopted by Jesuit clerics in Japan who taught him Japanese and the culture of the land. He remembered being impressed by how Yasuke became an accomplished samurai in a foreign land.

Menzi recalled studying Yasuke and being astounded by his social upward mobility. He wondered if he would ever be capable of overcoming obstacles in the same way the black samurai had. Yasuke was born in Africa but was taken to Japan as a slave and became a samurai of great renown.

The story of Yasuke's life was as remarkable to historians that studied it as it was mysterious. And then the sobering thought returned to him that he was in a situation in which he had no choice but to overcome.

"Attack!" yelled a commander on the side opposing the one Yasuke was on. Menzi immediately retreated further into the trees, trying his best to avoid being found out by anyone in that time period.

The two groups charged at each other, belting out battle cries as their katanas clashed. Menzi ducked until he was lying on the ground flat on his stomach. He covered his ears as he heard sounds like cannons and the screams of battle.

The rancid smell of gunpowder was in the air. Menzi could hear the clang of swords crossing and colliding. The din of conflict got so loud around Menzi that it proved futile for him to try and avoid it any further.

Menzi's heart pounded as the bedlam ensued around him. He began panting desperately as he felt panic hog room in his chest. He felt throbbing at his temples as his head started to ache with distress. As with many other moments since this adventure began, Menzi was at a loss for what to do.

It slowly dawned on Menzi that if he continued to hide, there was no way that he would accomplish the mission that he travelled to the 1500s to see through. He stiffened his face with resolve and picked himself up off the ground.

He stood at the ready, still in the brush, watching samurai cross swords and do battle for the final frontier between the men of Yasuke's mentor, Oda Nobunaga, and the forces of Nobunaga's arch-nemesis Takeda Katsuyori.

Regiments tasked with carrying long lance-like weapons were on the field with archers on either side of the battle, but the close proximity between belligerents meant that katanas were the weapon of choice for combat.

Menzi placed his finger on a button on the wrist of his Nommo armour. A large, silver shield materialised along Menzi's right arm that resembled the fin of an armoured fish. A retractable glowing blade also materialised on Menzi's left hand. A helmet materialised around his head.

He transformed from his Nommo form to his human form, with his skin going from scaly and green to

91

smooth and brown, his pupils going from vertical to round and the gills and fins on his forearms and neck vanishing.

The last thing Menzi wanted to do was startle any feudal Japanese warriors by emerging as an alien. It was bad enough that he was going to emerge with a futuristic battle armour with weapons the Japanese could not even imagine.

Menzi was working off a rule of thumb, but he suspected that it was best to influence as little as possible while he was in the distant past, especially during a significant military campaign which was documented and preserved for centuries by historians.

Nobody noticed as Menzi ran out into the melee of the battle. He raised his shield up high as he charged forward. He noticed Yasuke was fending off attacks from three men from Katsuyori's regiments.

Menzi gave a swipe of his laser blade, which gave enough kinetic energy to push all three of the men attacking Yasuke back. Yasuke turned around and noticed Menzi and froze for a moment. Menzi looked back at the black samurai.

"Behind you!" Menzi shouted. Yasuke immediately turned around and swiped at two attackers from Katsuyori's forces. Menzi was silently impressed by how well Yasuke was able to handle a sword, especially against men who knew the way of the samurai for longer than he did.

Yasuke turned around until he was facing Menzi. The young Nommo started to panic, thinking that Yasuke might have mistaken him for an enemy. Yasuke pulled a small sphere like object out of a point inside of his armour and forcefully threw it to the ground.

The dome let out streaks of purple light which grew until they engulfed Yasuke and Menzi in a sphere-like web, excluding everyone else on the battlefield. This stunned Menzi as he looked around at the sphere that he was in.

The dome was composed of a network of glowing purple lines, shapes, and figures. While the dome was semi-transparent, it appeared to create a hard boundary between the two and the rest of the battlefield. Everything outside of the dome seemed suspended in time.

"Wait. How did you do that?" Menzi asked, amazed by what he just witnessed the black samurai do. Yasuke put his katana back in its saya and gave Menzi a hostile stare. He walked up to Menzi until he was right in front of the young Nommo, towering over him.

"So Elder Amma has decided to send a warrior to me, as we discussed," Yasuke remarked as he looked Menzi in the eyes with a warm and amused look. Menzi's jaw dropped at what Yasuke had just said.

"So, you know about the Nommo? You know about Elder Amma and planet Nibiru and everything? In the 1500s? How is that even possible," Menzi marvelled. Yasuke's eyes hooded as he looked back at Menzi.

"I'm guessing by all of these questions that nobody on planet Nibiru briefed you, young Nommo. Something serious must have happened for Elder Amma to send someone back as out of sorts as you. And yes, I know Elder Amma very well. I am a Nommo, like you," Yasuke remarked.

Menzi held his head. "A recorded figure in earth's history was a Nommo? I'm sorry, I'm going to need to lie down after hearing this. I seriously thought I was the only one. This is incredible," Menzi extolled.

"Wow, you must have missed a lot of orientation classes, young Nommo! I suppose that you're here to get the artifact from me. That's fine. But I'm going to need to you to make yourself scarce and carry on with your mission after that. I'm in the middle of something important here," Yasuke said.

Yasuke pulled out a small double edged knife called a Tanto in its casing and handed it to Menzi. "And I believe you have something for me," Yasuke said, expecting Menzi to acquiesce by giving him the katana he received from the Zeta Reticuli.

"I have so many questions! Why send all of these Nommo to planet Earth? Why send me to planet Earth? And how many Nommos have lived on earth over the centuries? Are there more?" a staggered Menzi asked.

Yasuke held out the Tanto in front of Menzi. Menzi stared back. Yasuke briefly waved it around with haste, indicating that he wanted Menzi to take it. Menzi stepped forward and took the weapon out of Yasuke's hand.

"Elder Amma has placed Nommo warriors on Earth for thousands of years. The Nommo send warriors to many different planets across the universe to serve as protectors of young civilisations. We remain relatively unknown, with only the Dogon tribe interacting openly with us. All Nommo tend to know our origins and our mission from birth, but for some reason, I get the sense that you need to be brought up to speed on some things," Yasuke said.

"I'm not sure why, but I can't remember anything about being a Nommo. I only discovered that I was a Nommo a couple of days ago – into the future, I mean – when I found a baby in the streets and a UFO caused an explosion in my home city. That baby was the Positive Logos," Menzi recollected.

Menzi looked down at the Tanto in his hands and let out a sigh. Yasuke placed his hand on Menzi's shoulder. Menzi looked up at the black samurai and saw compassion in his eyes atypical of a battle worn warrior.

"If a farmer spends his hours fretting about whether he can sow seeds, he steals time from himself for reaping. You might not feel worthy of being entrusted with completing this mission, but Elder Amma sent you here, back to me, for a reason. The fate of the universe is at stake. I doubt she would have bothered with you if she did not believe that you could save us," Yasuke said.

Menzi nodded dutifully. He looked around outside of the sphere that he and Yasuke were in at the scene of war suspended in time. The warring samurai stayed in position, motionless. "Are they going to stay like that for long?" Menzi inquired awkwardly.

"They'll stay that way for as long as I need them to," Yasuke quipped. "But I need you to understand that even though you are doing this on your own, you can see this mission through. From here, you will need to find two other Nommo warriors in different time periods. You will need to collect some items from them too. By the time you finish your mission, you will be able to return to your present day. From there, it's up to you to save us. And you might need some of these," he added.

Yasuke reached into his armour again and pulled out a pouch. He placed it in Menzi's hands and the young Nommo opened it up and peeked inside. It was filled with small balls, similar to the one that Yasuke used to apparently stop time in the middle of the battlefield.

"Thank you, Yasuke. It was an honour to meet you and to learn that I have something in common with such a great historical figure. I will do my best to finish the mission. I won't let you down," Menzi extoled.

Yasuke smiled at Menzi, now with both his hands holding onto Menzi's shoulders firmly. "I have no doubt, young Nommo. Go and get it done. We need you. Now if you don't mind, I need to get back to today's order of business. Use one of those balls to hide form sight when you arrive at your next destination and, for goodness' sake, don't meddle in the course of history," Yasuke said.

Menzi nodded. Yasuke stepped away from Menzi and assumed his battle position. Menzi looked down at the Tanto again. "What do I do with these artifacts once I've collected all of them," Menzi asked Yasuke.

"You'll know what you need to do once the mission is done," Yasuke replied as he pulled his katana out, ready to resume with the battle. "Now if you don't mind, I'd appreciated

it if you went on your way, while I continue here and think up how to explain this away to anyone who might have seen you," he asked.

Menzi immediately pulled out the silver herb and set it alight. As it burned, Menzi called out to the Nommo and Elder Amma. Like it did at the Zeta Reticuli cosmic brain, a portal took shape in front of Menzi and opened up to take him to his next destination.

Menzi stood up and walked towards the portal. "Menzi!" Yasuke shouted as he began to walk in. Menzi stopped midstride and turned to Yasuke. "Good luck, young Nommo," Yasuke beamed at Menzi as he readied himself to resume with combat.

Menzi nodded with a smile. He turned to the portal, with its grey cloud-like smoke formations and small, dazzling lightning bolts. Menzi stepped in with the Tonto that Yasuke had just gifted him in hand.

As Menzi disappeared into the portal, Yasuke reached his hand out as the ball he had thrown on the grown to suspend time in the middle of the battle whizzed back into his palm and took shape once again.

The forcefield that materialised around Yasuke and Menzi vanished and the glowing purple lines and shames that punctuated the forcefield's border were gone. The melee of the battle continued with all of its blades, blood, and war cries.

Yasuke marked his eyes on two samurai charging at him from the same direction and positioned himself for defence and a counterattack. "Don't let us down, young Nommo," Yasuke said under his voice. "The universe needs you…"

CHAPTER 6: Sisters at War

Location: KwaZulu Natal, Planet Earth, current day

The regiments of the Andromedan army on earth had moved their mothership from the lagoon in the Indian Ocean to Mount Ntlenyana in the Drakensberg. The sprawling, metallic mothership sat motionless at the top of the mountain while most of the soldiers were outside of it.

Some of the Andromedan soldiers were preparing food at a nearby fire, while others trained in marksmanship, combat, and overall fitness. Others still were taking the time to admire the scenery during the welcomed reprieve from battle.

The Mathra mothership that was floating in the air before had phased away from Earth's orbit. Innozia sat on a large rock in a meditative state, looking up in the sky where the Mathra mothership once was. No one dared to interrupt the unflinching, stoic warrior princess.

Innozia's highest ranking general, Nammid, sat a short distance off with Taheeq, as they speculated about what was going through Innozia's mind. Taheeq turned and saw a hibiscus flower in the bushes. His eyes gave off a purple glow and the flower vanished in a purple glow immediately.

He turned back to Nammid with a smile. He opened his right palm and as a purple glow appeared in his palm - the same flower that disappeared from the bushes materialised in his hand. Taheeq revealed the flower to the Andromedan general who beamed back at the Pleiadian warrior.

"As impressive as this is, I am very curious about why you couldn't have done that to stop the Mathra mothership before it vanished," Nammid quipped. Taheeq smiled back in a good sporting spirit.

"Well, you know anyone with an ability has a limit. Mine just so happens to be sentient organisms and massive spaceships as large as buildings," Taheeq retorted. Taheeq took the hibiscus flower and gently placed it in Nammid's hair.

Nammid exposed the side of her hair as she laughed lightly, allowing the Pleiadian to place the flower in between the fine orange tendrils on her head. Taheeq's glowing eyes looked longingly into Nammid's massive black eyes as Nammid gazed back.

"Sometimes, my mind wonders to a fantasy world where your people and my people can live together in sincere and true peace. No conventions, no treaties. Just the same harmony that you and I enjoy together," said Taheeq.

"Careful what you ask for, soldier. You're not the only person with limited abilities here," Nammid said. "As much as I feel like the Andromedan Empire could be running their affairs better, my allegiance is to the Queen of Andromeda, first and foremost," she added.

Taheeq smiled. "Do you mean the Queen of Andromeda that is sitting on that rock right there a few feet away from us? Or do you mean the Queen of Andromeda that has seized the throne in your home city and might have just put a bounty on her own sister's head?" Taheeq asked.

Nammid hummed at Taheeq's question, with no reply. She instead turned to Taheeq and touched his bald, purple head. "I really hope we can come out from under all of this when this war is finally over," she sighed.

Taheeq embraced the Andromedan war general.

Mogoma walked up to the two aliens, who turned around to acknowledge him. "Has anyone seen any changes? I'm trying to reach out to Kwataar, and I cannot pick up his lifeforce signature anywhere in the cosmos," Mogoma said.

"Oh, no," fretted a concerned Nammid as she stood up. Nammid stepped closer to Mogoma and Taheeq followed right behind her. Mogoma had a confused look on his face, leaving the Andromedan and the Pleiadian to fear the worst. "Does that mean...?" Nammid paused.

"I don't think so. I've felt lifeforces extinguish many times and that is not what happened here. His lifeforce signature went from present, to distant, to just...just...vanishing," Mogoma said, at a loss to explain or make sense of what he was experiencing.

"But that's good, right? It means that there is a chance that he's still alive?" Nammid inquired.

"I'm quite confused by all of this. Elder Amma's lifeforce has indeed been extinguished, after her encounter with Natiki. She is gone," Mogoma said with a pause. Taheeq and Nammid looked on Mogoma with pity.

"But all indications seem to suggest that Kwataar and the Positive Logos are no longer with the Mathra. So, we can conclude that the Architect has not yet combined the Positive Logos with the Negative Logos. I just can't seem to make out where Kwataar is," Mogoma lamented.

Taheeq suddenly began to emit a bright glow throughout his body as he levitated. Nammid and Mogoma jolted as the Pleiadian glowed and floated unexpectedly. The two stood around Taheeq, realising the Pleiadians on Kappess moon were communicating with him, as others gathered.

The ten foot, lion-like alien Smeggar approached the trio, curious about what was happening. "Did he get one of those brightly coloured mushrooms? Menzi warned me that not all of them were edible," Smeggar inquired.

Princess Innozia noticed the commotion out of the corner off her eye. The Princess got up to approach her soldiers gathering around Taheeq, so that she could investigate further. Taheeq started to descend from mid-air as the glow of his body dimmed back to his normal purple skinned state.

"What's happening?" Innozia demanded as she arrived at the group. Nammid got closer to Taheeq, attempting to offer comfort as the Pleiadian caught his breath. Taheeq looked up at the Andromedan soldiers around him.

"It's from Kappess moon. They have just told me that the Positive Logos is with them. They say they are also under no illusions about the Mathra and are certain that they are on their way to Kappess to take the Positive Logos from them," Taheeq explained.

Innozia buried her face in her open palms with frustration. "This is just what I need. The Positive Logos is not in my possession and now my enemies are on the way to retrieve it in another galaxy, and I am the last to know?"

"I'm afraid the day is about to get a lot worse," Mogoma interjected. Everyone turned to Mogoma for him to elaborate. He did not say a word further but looked up into the skies. Everyone else looked up as well.

The Andromedan soldiers saw a pattern of round blue lights cut through overcast clouds in the sky as a massive spaceship was entering the earth's atmosphere. As the clouds cleared out of the spaceship's way, the Andromedan coat of arms came in view among its lights.

The Andromedan soldiers on the top of Mount Ntlenyana stood motionless, staring at the gigantic flying object slowly pushing through the clouds. "Is that...?" Smeggar started.

"It's my sister, Princess Natiki," Innozia said flatly. "I need everyone to get into formation. We are going to stand our ground and not give an inch. We are not engaging with allies. I repeat, we are not engaging with allies!" Innozia ordered.

The soldiers of the Andromedan army on ground took to their positions and held their weapons at the ready. Innozia's spaceship was closed up and secured. Taheeq levitated in a battle stance, ready for combat. Nammid pulled out her laser blade. Smeggar bore his long claws.

The projectile force from Natiki's spaceship caused winds that blew in all directions as Innozia's soldiers struggled to maintain their balance. A doorway opened on the ship as it descended, revealing Natiki standing between two advisors and in front of a huge army.

Natiki stood with her arms crossed and a smug smile broke on her face as she looked down on the mountain top to see her older sister Innozia. Princess Innozia scowled back at her sister with her laser blade in hand.

"This is quite a predicament that we are in, Princess," whispered Nammid, standing right next to Innozia.

"You think?" Innozia retorted.

"So, her coronation was a few Andromeda days ago. If we stand against her, this makes us enemies of the Andromedan crown. Are we fugitives right now, as we speak?" Nammid asked.

"Let me worry about the palace intrigue," said the battle-tested warrior princess, Innozia. "We stand our ground with the authority that is given to us by the Andromedan Empire. As for my sister, the queen, she cannot continue her duties without a head intact, and in that event, they will fall to me."

Natiki's ship was now close enough that she jumped off of it and landed on the ground, a fair distance off. Nammid gulped. Mogoma allowed his fin blades to protrude from her forearms, ready for battle.

So confident in her security in front of Innozia and her soldiers behind her was Natiki that she was the only Andromedan from her delegation to leave her mothership. She slowly started walking towards Innozia and her soldiers.

"My sister!" Natiki exclaimed as she got closer to Innozia. Natiki belted out a loud, hearty laugh as she opened up her arms still walking towards Innozia. Innozia's soldiers started to walk towards Natiki as she approached Innozia. "Stand down," Innozia ordered. Her soldiers stood back.

Innozia retracted her laser blade, still not taking her eyes off of Natiki. The two daughters of Oyo Seviv were reunited for the first time since her untimely death. While Natiki smiled at her older sister, Innozia kept a scowl that likely betrayed violent intentions.

"I really thought you would be happier to see me, sister. You know, the death of a matriarch can really take its toll on a family and I've heard it is important that survivors of such a death become much more intentional about maintaining connection, or the family will fall apart! Hug?" Natiki offered with open arms.

"Nah, I'm good," Innozia said, seething anger still marked on her face. Natiki leaned back slightly, feigning shock that her sister would spurn a request for an embrace. Innozia's fists clenched even tighter as Natiki's smile turned from smug to bemused. "It was worth a try," she shrugged with a smile.

Countless soldiers from Natiki's militia were streaming off of her mothership and followed her to her encounter with Innozia and her soldiers. Nammid noticed that they had fast become outnumbered in the standoff.

Natiki's decorous pretence suddenly melted away as she was now scowling like her sister. "Not that you could ever be happy for me, but it's been an exciting journey so far, being the new Queen of Andromeda," Natiki said to Innozia matter-of-factly.

"Oh, I can imagine," Innozia replied. "Especially given how fast you've been moving with the succession procedures, you know. Really throwing the rule book out of the window," she added.

"Yes, well, you know I've never been a fan of tradition for its own sake," Natiki huffed back. "Innozia, I had to do something. You had abandoned your post, galivanting around in the rural backwoods of the universe without even recovering the Logos," Natiki gestured at their surroundings with disdain.

"I just want to know why..." Innozia said.

"Why did I assume a throne that I was entitled to after our mother's passing when our people needed leadership, while you were preoccupied with exploits of the frontier? Is that what you're asking me?" Natiki asked rhetorically.

"I want to know why you murdered our mother, if I may be so blunt as to ask...your majesty," Innozia said as a single tear fell from her eye and trickled away in the wind. The tension at the top of the mountain heightened. Natiki looked back at Innozia as her scowl grew darker.

"There you go," Natiki said. "Your empire was on the brink of collapse as recently as a few Andromeda days ago, and all you can do is think about yourself and the past and how things were. I thank the stars you didn't succeed our mother. You would have just held us back," she said as her eyes watered.

"I was here on duty! Our mother sent me here!" Innozia exploded. "And while I was honouring her

111

wishes, you plotted against your own family and staged a coup! You have the gall to tell me that I'm thinking about myself?" she hissed.

"This is no coup, Innozia. I belong to the royal family too. My claim to the throne is no less valid than yours! In fact, I am more of a royal that you could ever hope to be. I am the Queen of Andromeda!" Natiki screamed.

"And anyway, you didn't have it in you to do what our empire needed you to do. Look at you," Natiki gestured at her sister's battle-worn armour. "You don't even have the Logos with you, do you? Outsmarted by those Mathra cockroaches! And you wanted to be queen," Natiki scoffed.

"At least I knew how the legitimate queen wanted the Logos to be handled. She wanted it kept safe from the hands of anyone with nefarious intentions to misuse its incredible powers. Like you," Innozia replied.

Natiki frowned at Innozia's rebuttal in silence for a moment. She then let out a loud maniacal laugh. Other than the howl from a mighty gust of wind, Natiki's guffaw was the only thing that could be heard on the tense battlefield.

"Share the joke, sister," Innozia said with a stoic scowl. Natiki doubled over as she caught her breath from the genuine but disdainful laugh. Once she was standing upright again, she motioned her open palm in Innozia's direction. "It's you, sister," Natiki responded. "You're the joke".

"Think about it, Innozia. Look at the Andromedan Empire, in all of its glory. Over nine million settlements, across seven hundred thousand galaxies and billions of stars. These worms you call your allies have barely mastered exploiting all of the power on their home planet. They cling to that tiny yellow star in the sky for everything they have while we pick entire stars out of the sky on a whim like cherries and mine them for power. Do you honestly think that this was all achieved from humanitarian aid and being of service to lesser civilisations? You're kidding yourself! And so was our mother," Natiki said.

"I don't want to hear it," Innozia snapped as she turned her head to the side. Natiki tilted her head, knowing she struck a nerve with her older sister. She walked closer to her sister until she was right in front of Innozia and could not be ignored. Innozia turned and faced Natiki again.

"We have a responsibility to this universe. It's not just a plaything we can just tinker with for our own amusement. Our history is not stainless, but we understand our role in making the circumstances of life in this universe better. Or at least mother did," Innozia chastised.

"The circumstances we find ourselves in are not my fault. I am not responsible for the empire that you and I were born into. But when you see this farce of peace and concord that you treasure crumble into dust; when every star in the sky is under the power of Andromeda; when we have no need to negotiate with other empires because we are the only one left; when you see the Andromedan Empire become more powerful than any of its founders could have ever imagined, you will have no one to blame for that but me," Natiki declared.

"SHUT UP!" Innozia blurted out as she drew and activated her laser blade. Natiki smiled before activating the imperial battle armour that belonged to her and Innozia's mother. Innozia momentarily flinched as she saw the familiar regalia materialise on Natiki's body before charging at her sister.

Natiki's soldiers took the cue and got into attack. Innozia's soldiers were already at the ready and pounced to Innozia's defence, creating a scrimmage. Two Andromedan militias were now in battle against one another.

One mighty leap carried Innozia until she was right in front of Natiki. Innozia raised her arm to swing the laser blade at Natiki's neck. Natiki swiftly ducked the swipe from the skilled warrior princess with a rapid sidestep until her hand was directly aimed at Innozia's back.

The left arm guard on Natiki's armour shimmered again until a photon cannon appeared on Natiki's hand. Natiki flashed a sadistic smile as the photon cannon lit up to fire. The fast and agile Innozia quickly turned around and her eyes dilated at the sight of the photon energy.

Innozia's peerless reflexes kicked in and she desperately jumped up to dodge the photon blast until her feet were in the air above Natiki's head. Natiki reached out and grabbed Innozia's lower leg while her sister was in mid-air and dragged her down until Innozia hit the ground on her back.

Before Innozia could get a chance to writhe in pain, Natiki was already stomping on her torso repeatedly. Innozia caught Natiki's foot mid-stomp and twisted her ankle until she fell over. Innozia climbed over Natiki until she was looking over her sister's face and dealing her multiple punches.

Elsewhere on the battlefield Mogoma was firing blasts at multiple Andromedan soldiers in Natiki's militia, but even amongst the few that were affected by the shots, two always seemed to pop up and take the place of the one taken down.

Taheeq used his telepathic powers to defend himself from the onslaught. He attempted to use his abilities to hurl boulders and blasts in the direction of soldiers attacking him. But the Andromedan soldiers were so fast that they easily dodged every attempt at an attack.

As Andromedan war general, Nammid, was more adept at defending an attack from Andromedan soldiers than her fellow soldiers who were not ethnic Andromedans. However, even she was getting snowed under in the overwhelming number of soldiers that targeted and attacked her.

Natiki continued to try and escape from under Innozia and her relentless punches. She activated her mother's imperial battle armour once again, causing a helmet to phase over her head to shield it from Innozia's vicious shots.

Natiki managed to position her left hand under Innozia's abdomen at just the right position before the

116

armour caused the photon blaster to phase onto her left arm. Natiki's photon cannon let off an overwhelming photon blast, whose impact sent Innozia flying off of her.

Innozia's body flipped some eighteen feet into the air. Before Innozia could hit the ground, Natiki sprang up and a matter-shifting device phased onto the end of her right arm. Natiki used this to shoot a beam at Innozia.

Instead of harming her, the beam suspended Innozia in the air as Natiki aimed at her. As Natiki moved her arm, Innozia's position in the air shifted. She moved her arm, shifting Innozia's body as it phased into a nearby boulder until only her head was peeking out.

Innozia looked down at the boulder that her body had just been encased in from the neck down and gritted her teeth as she struggled to break out. Natiki slowly walked towards the boulder Innozia was trapped in as her helmet retracted to reveal that she had a sinister smile on her face.

"AGATALA!" Natiki screamed, ordering her soldiers to suspend their attack. Natiki's soldiers stopped their attack, already confident that they had overwhelmed Innozia's soldiers. Innozia's militia stopped fighting after seeing Innozia's position, cautious not to endanger her.

All the soldiers looked on at the warring royal sisters as the battlefield fell tense and quiet. Nammid looked on, wanting to intervene, but noticed Natiki's weapons were retracting into her armour and reconsidered.

"How convenient is this?" Natiki yelled with a maniacal laugh. "Tell me, sister. Who's the big girl of the palace now?" Natiki taunted.

"I swear on my mother's blood, I will kill you!" Innozia seethed as she struggled to break free from the boulder that her body was stuck in. Natiki laughed in her sister's face as tears began to well up in Innozia's eyes.

"Now, now, Innozia," Natiki feigned shock. "You are in no position to be making threats when you are at my mercy at this very moment. I would suggest you pick your next words very carefully," Natiki warned.

"I cannot let you do this. You have one more chance to stop this madness," Innozia fumbled as Natiki looked her right in the eyes.

"You have missed the boat, haven't you? I am in control now. My scout has just radioed me to inform me that the Positive Logos and Negative Logos are no longer on this planet. You failed. But while your failure is fatal, it is not yet final. No. I want you alive to watch me become the most powerful Andromedan queen that has ever lived. I want you to marvel at the magnitude of your failure and the full glory of my majesty!" Natiki exclaimed.

Natiki turned around and raised her hands, as if putting on a performance of her victory. Her mothership came in view, hovering over the soldiers on the battlefield. Natiki turned back to Innozia with a scowl. She leaned in to whisper into Innozia's ear.

"Well, I've got to run now. I have some important things to do. But don't worry sister. We will see each other again. And when we do, I will put you exactly where I put our dearest mother," Natiki whispered.

Innozia immediately let out a hellish scream of rage and pain. Natiki turned around and walked towards her mothership without skipping a beat as her sister screamed behind her. Natiki's soldiers followed her into the ship.

The mothership levitated into a higher altitude for several seconds until it blasted off out of the atmosphere, almost as quickly as it had arrived. Innozia's soldiers were left behind, licking their wounds after a punishing battle.

Innozia strained and screamed until the boulder her body was trapped in began to crack. Smeggar approached Innozia and dug his massive hands into the cracks and broke the boulder open to free the Andromedan princess.

Nammid ran to the highest peak at the top of the mountain and fired at the departing mothership, trying to shoot it down with a plasma pistol in vain. Taheeq looked up at the skies the ship disappeared into, stoic and emotionless.

"We should have stopped her," Innozia said dusting off her armour as she sat on the ground. No one dared respond to the princess, although it was clear that the decision not to attack Natiki was made for Innozia's own safety.

"The Positive Logos is on Kappess moon. She knows that it's there. And that's where she's headed," said Taheeq, still looking up to the sky.

"Well, she's in for a surprise once she gets there. The Pleiadians are already defending the Positive Logos and the Mathra are also on their way there," Mogoma reasoned.

"My brothers on Kappess moon are capable warriors, despite their pacifist values. They will be able to put up a fight against the Mathra and the Andromedans, but only for so long. We are going to have to follow them to Kappess," said Taheeq.

"Are we on course to do that immediately?" Innozia asked, turning to Nammid. Nammid checked the mothership's status on a body device and hesitate when the data appeared to her.

"The ship will still require several hours to charge up for the journey to Kappess, but we should be able to leave for that region right after that," Nammid said. Innozia huffed at Nammid's response.

Innozia struggled back up to her feet and began limping past her soldiers and towards her mothership. Innozia's soldiers continued nursing their wounds as they realised that the battle had only just begun in earnest.

"Alright, soldiers. That does it. Once we have the supplies and the fuel, we're going to Kappess moon to retrieve the Positive Logos and take the Negative Logos from the Mathra. And everyone had better make sure they steer clear of Princess Natiki. I will kill her myself," Innozia brooded.

CHAPTER 7: Incendiary dreams

Location: on the edge of the Milky Way, on the way to Kappess Moon

The Mathra mothership advanced on through the stars on its way to the Pleiadian sanctuary on Kappess Moon to locate and find the Positive Logos. The Architect was becoming increasingly accustomed to the powers of the Negative Logos which he had allowed to bond with his body.

The Negative Logos enhanced the Architect's abilities significantly. He had the power to increase the coverage of distance by the Mathra mothership. The Negative Logos did this by warping space and matter ahead of it to reduce the distance between the mothership and its destination.

The advanced technology of the Andromedans could not hope to give them an advantage this great in pursuit of the Logos. The Architect was closer than ever to realising his life's mission of cosmic conquest and he knew it.

He was in his supreme chambers in the mothership, surrounded only by the Mathra of highest rank, including masons, sculptors, and welders. The other

Mathra continued working dutifully and fearfully to help the Architect's vision come to reality.

The hierarchy of the Mathra campaign remained intact in the face of resistance from the Nommo and the Andromedans. The Architect was convinced that the centre would hold against the Pleiadians.

"Sculptors. I need an estimated time of arrival and an assessment of the terrestrial environment, level of threat and proximity of the threat to the Positive Logos," the Architect brooded to his hive of fearful, loyal servants.

"We should be arriving in the orbit of Kappess Moon within a matter of minutes, Architect. A scan of terrestrial activity detects no military mobilisation in anticipation for our arrival. The threat to our campaign should be minimal," said a sculptor, scanning through screen monitors with its insectoid eyes.

"Excellent!" exclaimed the Architect. The Negative Logos, attached to the left side of his abdomen, began to give off a deep red glow and the Architect winced in suppressed agony. The surrounding Mathra continued on with their work, feigning ignorance at their master's discomfort.

"Master Architect, would you like us to assess you with regard to the discomfort you have been feeling since the Negative Logos was bonded with your body?" one Mathra welder asked nervously, breaking the tense silence.

"What makes you think I am experiencing any discomfort?" the Architect asked. The control room on the Mathra mothership fell silent. Others in the control room could hear an audible gulp in the midst of the tension. The welder fixed itself up to respond, as its feet meandered nervously for balance.

"I fear the cosmic energy contained in the Negative Logos is causing you to fall ill, perhaps corrupting your senses. It is becoming harder to ascertain what instructions stem from your will and which ones come from hostile spirits outside of your control," the welder stammered.

The tension in the control room intensified as no one dared chime in, knowing how wrathful and dangerous the Architect was, particularly now that he was so close to accomplishing his mission. The welder huffed, halfway incredulous, halfway frightened.

"It boggles my mind that I would have to state this to you, welder, but no one on this ship is in control but me. You would do well to remember that if you do not want retribution to fall upon you. I cannot allow insurrection in my ranks at this crucial part of my plan," the Architect said.

The welder gulped. "I thought this was about freeing the Mathra race after millions of years of oppression and marginalisation. But the closer we get to accomplishing this mission, the more I hear you talk about your plans, your ambitions and what is due to you," the welder said.

"And...?" the Architect goaded.

No one in the control room dared to make a sound. The welder looked down at the control room floor. A small number of the Mathra strategists left the control room, sensing that this exchange would end badly.

"What is it to you if I would prefer to be the only living thing left after I have shredded this universe down to its last atom?" the Architect asked rhetorically.

"I would simply like to know what the benefit is for the Mathra if this campaign is about your own conquest and we are but a mere afterthought. You united us because we were in agreement that the Andromedans oppressed us, and they had to be destroyed. We united behind you because we believed that you were our liberator. But if you have no interest in liberating us, then we have not truly been liberated. We have merely exchanged one oppressor for another that looks like us," the welder reasoned.

The remaining Mathra in the control room shifted their gaze from the audacious welder to their leader, the Architect.

"I need not gratify your defiance with a response. I will lead this mission on my terms, and I will not be answerable to any of you, least of all insurrectionists with no sense of loyalty to the interests of the Mathra," the Architect admonished.

The welder shuddered and looked down at the control room floor. The Architect walked up the welder until he was standing right in front of it. The Architect looked down at the welder and gave it a menacing smirk.

"This is unforgivable. You will have to be punished," the Architect said dispassionately.

Two mason Mathra stepped forward with sceptres, with slight hesitation on their faces. The sceptres had a spark at the end of them and were able to rip through flesh effortlessly. The protesting welder wept.

The Architect turned around and left the control room, with little more sign of the deadly scene than hellish screams from the welder and flashes of light from the weapons that were ripping his body apart. The Architect was now resolute. His mission and its successful end was clear. He would not be disappointed, and he would not be challenged.

Chapter 8: Remember...

Location: Kingdom of Ndongo, Angola, 1630.

The dark clouds and sparks of lightning that accompanied Menzi's teleportation appeared in the open plains of the Ndongo kingdom. They formed a doorway in thin air, through which Menzi walked out from feudal Japan and walked into Angola in the 1600s.

He walked into a vibrant and busy gathering where drums where thundering through the area with songs and melodies sung by almost all in attendance. It was not immediately clear to him where he was, but he knew that he was back on the African continent.

Nobody immediately took note of him, but he saw that he was in the presence of a heavy battle contingent because most of the individuals around him, men, and women alike, carried shields, spears and battle axes.

The sun above him beat hot and heavy on his brow. He looked around at the people around him noticing that they wore animal hides, headgear and wrist and ankle bangles, but were all also topless. The drumming and singling got louder as it gathered pace.

Suddenly he remembered the voice he heard when he was teleported away from the Mothra mothership and to the planet of the Zeta Reticuli. After having met Yasuke in Japan, it stood to reason that Menzi was either in Angola in the 1600 or he was in the Mali Empire in the 1500s.

He was inside of an enclosure that was marked off by a fence made from crooked sticks of wood and thick tree branches. He could hear the crackle of a large bonfire nearby and he picked up the strong scent of something fermented being brewed, likely a type of alcohol.

The sky was overcast, with a smoking tinge of orange, indicating that it was either in the evening or the fire nearby was so great that its smoking was obscuring a clear view of the sky, including a pristine peach sunset.

In the middle of the noise on the scene, he felt a firm hand behind him shoving his right shoulder. He staggered forward in three quick steps, careful not to lose his balance and fall. He turned around to see who shoved him.

In front of him, he saw a tall warrior standing and waiting to spar. The warrior stared right into Menzi's eyes, although the young Nommo warrior tried his best to avoid eye contact. The warrior raised his spear and pointed it in Menzi's direction, indicating his intention to fight.

Menzi looked down at the Tonto blade that Yasuke gave to him. He grabbed onto the Tonto blade tight and closed his eyes. The Tonto blade began to give off a blue glow that soon covered Menzi's body completely. The energy from the glow gave off a gentle wave of energy.

The warrior antagonising Menzi took a step back. Blue beams of light started surrounding Menzi, until they created the visage of extended arms on Menzi's body which were each three inches longer than his physical arms and were much larger in size.

Menzi looked at the hologram-like appendages that appeared on either side of him. He used them to reach down and grab a handful of dirt. The hand on the left holographic arm grabbed the dirt and scooped it up from the ground. Menzi also had a blue glow in his eyes.

Menzi turned to the warrior as he clenched the large glowing arms that were now on his body. The gathering started to surround Menzi and the warrior as the spectacle developed. "This is your last chance to step back. I don't want to hurt you," Menzi warned.

The warrior did not take kindly to the warning at all. Instead, he let out a hellish scream and charged at Menzi. Menzi reacted immediately swiped his spear away and used the massive glowing arms that appeared on him to deal a mean right fist to the attacker. The warrior was sent flying back ten meters.

More warriors started screaming and attacking Menzi. Menzi stood, ready to fight back with the powerful and esoteric weapons he got from the Nommo and Yasuke. Three warriors charged at him, and he successfully swiped one away as though they were a fly.

He gave two successive right punches to the remaining attackers and they fell back right away. Menzi turned around and saw another five attackers rushing at him all at once. He swiftly grabbed one in the left fist of the massive hands that he controlled and used him as a club to swipe the others away.

Another seven warriors charged at him from all directions, with three of the warriors being directly in front of him. He used the glowing hands to make a single forceful clap, which triggered a wave that sent them flying back.

Other warriors continued with their attack, trying to strike the large glowing hands, only to find that any attack they waged against the glowing, translucent limbs phased right through them as though they were apparitions.

Menzi showed the elbows of both of his large glowing arms in either direction, striking his attackers and shoving them back. Menzi stretched one of these hands out and spun swiftly, knocking out another dozen warriors that were assailing him.

Menzi saw that the onslaught was only getting larger with each attempt to attack him. It became clear to the young Nommo warrior that he would have to find a final and swift way to neutralise the attack. He looked to his left and then to his right before looking up to the sky.

Menzi then jumped up until he was some thirty feet in the arm. He raised the large glowing arms on his person above him and clenched their huge fists. He came barrelling back down to the ground and struck it with all of his might.

The force of his strike on the ground caused a vibration so great that it caused all of the warriors that were attacking him to lose their balance and hit the ground. He looked around as he saw the large, glowing, ethereal arms he conjured out of nowhere beginning to vanish.

The warriors that were resolute on ambushing Menzi just moments ago were so disoriented that they could not bring themselves to attempt another assault after they got themselves on two feet again. That is, except for one warrior who had just walked into the area.

The warrior yelled something to Menzi as he pointed his spear in the direction of the Nommo warrior, much like the first assailant did. Menzi turned around to face this last attacker, ready to defend himself.

"THAT'S ENOUGH!!!" screamed a voice in the distance.

Menzi turned his head. He saw a woman standing at an elevated platform, outside of the confined space that he was in. She wore a combination of fabrics and animal hide with a crown on her head. She stared at Menzi almost as if she were looking right through him.

"You! Up here," said the lady, summoning Menzi to leave the confined space and report to her. Menzi looked around himself at the warriors that were attacking him just a minute ago and noticed that they were clearing his path and indicating the way to get to the lady that called him closer.

Menzi walked in the direction indicated to him. He saw an open gate and a ramp that moved upwards to a platform. He began to walk up slowly, wondering who this mysterious lady was and whether he was still in danger.

Once he got to the top of the ramp he turned to his right and could see the lady more clearly and completely. She carried a battle axe in one hand and a shield in the other. She looked back at Menzi, almost as if to assess him for weapons. "Well? Come closer," the lady ordered.

Menzi reluctantly stepped closer to the lady. Once he was directly in front of her, he took to one knee, as a show of respect, realising that she had a lot of authority in the place that he found himself in. "On your feet," the lady said.

Menzi nervously adjusted himself until he was standing up straight. "I was sent here on a mission by the Nommo to find someone who has something to give me. Are you, by chance Queen Nzinga?" Menzi asked.

"Yes, I am Queen Nzinga. You must be sent here by Elder Amma," the queen said, unsurprised. Menzi's head cocked back slightly, startled that Queen Nzinga knew about the Nommo and Elder Amma. "Well, there's probably little time to waste. Follow me," the lady said.

Queen Nzinga walked in a direction away from the confined space Menzi was in. Menzi followed the queen. They walked away from the public square of the Ndongo kingdom and walked towards a large house at the centre of the settlement.

As they walked in, Menzi noticed the spear bearing warriors stationed at the doorway on either side, guarding the queen as she walked into her regal abode. They walked into the Ndongo imperial throne room. Nzinga took to her seat and pointed Menzi to a nearby stump.

Menzi obliged and took the seat. He looked around at weapons and shields mounted on the walls, as hallmarks of a throne room for a true warrior empress. He turned to Queen Nzinga and beamed a coy smiled.

"No point in an orientation, since you've already become acquainted with our...welcoming committee," the queen quipped. "So, tell me, young Nommo. To what do I owe the pleasure of this visit and how is Elder Amma doing?" Queen Nzinga asked as she smiled back at Menzi.

"Well, to be honest, I don't know Elder Amma all that well. I've never met her before. But make no mistake, things are rather urgent right now," Menzi admitted.

"Interesting," remarked the queen. "Care to fill me in?" she asked.

"Well, I was teleported away from present day while I had the Positive Logos with me, but when I came to, I was on another planet which was under the control of the Zeta Reticuli. They told me that Elder Amma told them about a back-up plan she had to stop the Mathra and since I was the closest Nommo around, it was up to me to make sure it worked. I was sent back in time on earth to meet up with Yasuke, you and, I'm guessing...Mansa Musa...?" Menzi explained.

"Yes, Elder Amma told me pretty much the same thing. She told me that if I encounter any Nommo, I should know that they were sent by her and that our efforts to keep harmony in the endless stars were in dire straits," Queen Nzinga said.

"If you don't mind me asking, how is it that an African queen is preoccupied with the exploits of building an empire all while having a mission to keep the entire universe safe in the back of her mind and a safely guarded secret that lasts for centuries?" Menzi asked.

"Elder Amma is my mother, as much as she is yours, young Nommo. But she has also given her children the freedom to lead the lives that most align to their individual truths. She is a remarkable spirit indeed. It is quite a shame that you haven't met her," Queen Nzinga remarked.

"I see," Menzi said. "This mission I'm on confuses me a great deal. The fact that we would align ourselves with the Andromedan Empire despite what they have done to the Mathra and other races. Why would we give Andromeda a pass after all of the wrong that they have done?" Menzi asked.

"It's good that you are thinking about this so deeply. The Nommo are committed to freedom. The oppression of the Mathra cannot be discounted and they are deserving of justice. What cannot be ignored is that the Architect's idea of justice is retributive and will happen at the destruction of all life in the universe. That is something the Nommo cannot allow," the queen explained.

Menzi nodded. "A lot of what you say rings true. Hatred cannot make right what was wrong. But hatred born out of injustice is hard to quell. Maybe if the universe were more just and fair, we wouldn't have to make such difficult decisions," Menzi wondered.

"Yes. But we don't live in a fantasy world. We live in this world...the real world," Queen Nzinga said flatly. She called for a servant to come into the room. The queen whispered instructions into the servant's ear and the servant dutifully walked over to the corner of the room.

The servant walked back to Queen Nzinga with a folded cheetah skin in hand. The servant brought a stump and placed it right in front of the queen. The servant placed the cheetah skin on the stump and unfolded it to reveal a Ndongo battle axe.

Queen Nzinga grabbed the battle-axe and held it up so that Menzi could see it. Menzi looked at the axe. It looked like the axes carried by the other warriors he had just seen, but had a black matte appearance to it, reflecting no light.

"This axe is made from metals from the Planet Nibiru. Its abilities are unlike any metal in this world. It is not as powerful as the Logos, but if used well in battle, it could give you a fighting chance to stop The Architect from combining the Positive Logos with the Negative Logos," Queen Nzinga explained.

Menzi took the axe, after hesitating for a moment. "The thing is, Queen Nzinga, I'm not like you. I haven't been reared to be a warrior my whole life. This whole thing is the first semblance I've had of a fight in my life. What if I'm not good enough to stop the Architect?" Menzi asked.

"Listen, child. If any one of us has a chance at stopping the architect, you have a chance at stopping the Architect," Queen Nzinga replied casually. "Besides, I just saw you make short work of Imbangala warriors before my very eyes, and they are no pushovers. Trust me, self-doubt is not an experience that is exclusive to you, young Nommo. I have a brother who has me doubting myself occasionally, and he is a fool," she said, smiling at Menzi.

Menzi smiled back half-heartedly. He took a long look at the battle-axe in his hands. "Thank you, Queen Nzinga. I will do my best not to let you down," Menzi said. Queen Nzinga smiled back at the young Nommo warrior.

The two stood up. The servant excused himself from the room, as Queen Nzinga motioned to him to give them some privacy. The servant stood up from his knees and left the room without thinking twice.

Menzi lit up the alloy herb, getting ready to create another portal. "If you get a chance to speak to Elder Amma one day, please send her my warmest regards," Queen Nzinga requested.

The portal burst open. Menzi turned back to Queen Nzinga and smiled, nodding at her request. "I don't know her as well as I would like to, but I am sure that Elder Amma remembers you," Menzi said to the queen.

Menzi tucked the battle-axe he had just received into a pouch and prepared to walk into the portal for the third and final stop in his journey. He stepped into the dark and purple ether of the portal as he heard the final words from Queen Nzinga.

"Don't mess this up, young Nommo...!"

CHAPTER 9: The Architect Arrives

Location: The Pleiadian sanctuary on the moon of Kappess

A small group of Pleiadians gathered at the great sanctuary of Kappess moon, tending to the Positive Logos that had just appeared amongst them hours before. The calm mood at the sanctuary was a stark contrast to the mood in other parts of the cosmos regarding the Mathra campaign.

The Pleiadian sanctuary on the moon of Kappess appeared as tranquil as ever. Plant life of all shapes, sizes, and colours could be seen in the holy garden. The sky had an ethereal purple haze to it with stars adorning the sky like sparkling ornaments on a gilded veil.

In the garden, Pleiadians were tending to their crops, while other Pleiadians meditated and conducted chants to align themselves with the cosmic energy around them. A nearby stream trickled gently from higher up on the hill where the sanctuary was located.

Despite the calm and picturesque exterior of Kappess moon, the people of Taheeq's native civilisation knew that the fate of the cosmos was in anything but safe hands. They also knew that the universe's fate depended on what they would do next.

Mogori watched over the Positive Logos as it lay sleeping peacefully in a makeshift cradle. Other Pleiadians were going about their daily business, fetching water from the nearby stream, tending to the vast plant life in the sanctuary and meditating and chanting for good fortunes.

Young Pleiadians could be heard playing and laughing near the stream, not thinking about the great battle ahead to keep the universe intact and safe. Tawa approached Mogori and stopped mere footsteps away from the Pleiadian elder.

Mogori raised his head but did not turn around to face Tawa. Still looking at Mogori and the Positive Logos, Tawa stood still a small distance behind the Pleiadian elder. Mogori already knew what Tawa wanted to discuss; the warning the entire camp recently received from Taheeq.

"Brother Taheeq said the Mathra are coming. We are going to need to get the children clear of the sanctuary and prepare to protect the Positive Logos from the

Mathra. We cannot allow the Architect to get his hands on it," Tawa said to Mogori.

"I am aware, brother Tawa," Mogori responded, still not looking at Tawa. The younger of the two Pleiadians was stunned at Mogori's reticent demeanour. Tawa walked closer to Mogori and grabbed onto his shoulder firmly.

"I fear that you are not taking this matter as seriously as you could be, Elder Mogori. We are about to come face to face with a power-hungry tyrant that wants to bring about an end to the universe as we know it and he is the closest he has ever been to accomplishing his mission," Tawa said.

Mogori turned around, looked Tawa in the eyes and said nothing. Tawa let go of Mogori's shoulder and took a step back from the elder. Mogori turned his head and looked at the Positive Logos again and sighed.

"There is nothing that we can do at this point, Tawa. Events have already gotten ahead of us," Mogori said. "We will be outnumbered by the Mathra once they come seeking the Positive Logos. And if they don't defeat us, the Andromedans will," Mogori lamented.

Mogori walked past Tawa and started slowly making his way to his cottage, turning his back to Tawa, yet again. Tawa followed behind Mogori, anxious to get his attention so they could discuss the coming emergency.

"But there has to be something that we can do!" Tawa said as the two walked towards Mogori's cottage. The stoic Mogori kept beating his path to the cottage did not respond to Tawa and his warning, only replying once they go to the privacy of the cottage.

"I understand your anxiety about the situation we find ourselves in, young Tawa," Mogori said as he took a seat in the cottage. "But I do not appreciate your fearmongering in front of your brothers in the sanctuary," he added.

"What am I supposed to do, Elder Mogori? The Architect and the Mathra are on their way here for the Positive Logos. And you are just folding your arms and saying that nothing can be done! What are the brothers of the sanctuary supposed to make of that?" Tawa asked.

"What is it to you if I want them to make exactly what I said of my utterances, brother Tawa? If we can both be honest to each other, this is not about saving the universe for you. This is about taking a position amongst the Pleiadians that you believe you deserve; a position that currently belongs to me," said Mogori.

The two suddenly turned to the west of the room that they were in. They both stared at a pschent-like headgear that sat on the elder seat. It belonged to the appointed leader of the Pleiadians. Tawa's face turned avaricious.

"You have not been in agreement with me about how the Pleiadians do things and how we involve ourselves in the matters of the cosmos for a long time, brother Tawa. I get the sense that your patience with me has finally run out," Mogori said.

"We have our differences, Elder Mogori. But all things considered, I am on your side," said Tawa. "We have different ideas about what is best for the Pleiadians and what is best for the cosmos, but we currently face a common enemy," he added.

"What would your position on me, and my leadership be if the cosmos were not teetering on the brink of

146

annihilation?" Mogori asked, now looking directly into Tawa's glowing blue eyes.

"We can get into this later, Elder Mogori," Tawa said. "What are we going to do once the Mathra arrive in the sanctuary?" he asked.

Mogori started walking towards the elder seat. "We will stand before them and tell them that we will not allow them to take the Positive Logos from us while a single Pleiadian on the sanctuary of Kappess moon is alive and breathing," said Mogori.

"Meaning that we will fight to the death to make sure that the Mathra do not take the Positive Logos from us? Even if we manage to defeat the Mathra, the Andromedans will be coming soon after and will do away with whatever is left of us," Tawa said.

"Exactly," Mogori said as he put on the pschent and sat on the elder seat. Tawa stared at Mogori and his nonchalant disposition, stunned to silence. Mogori stared back at him, saying nothing. Tawa marched to Mogori and stood right in front of the elder seat as the Mogori sat on it.

"It cannot just be as simple as that! There has to be something that we can do to defeat the Mathra and the Andromedans! We are Pleiadians. We are about hope and striving for a better future! We don't give up!" Tawa protested.

Mogori sat in silence and looked back at Tawa, who looked down at the elder enraged. Mogori stood up and stood face to face with Tawa. "I need to go out there and give our brothers their orders," said Mogori.

"Wait, Elder. What about the Positive Logos? We can use its power to defend ourselves from the Mathra and we will even have a fighting chance against the Andromedans. We have the perfect weapon right here. We just need to use it!" Tawa suggested.

"That is absolutely out of the question, brother Tawa. We are sworn to an oath to never use the Positive Logos to meet our own ends and gains. I have no intention of seeing that oath broken under my watch," Mogori said, dismissing Tawa's suggestion.

"Why not, Elder, Mogori? We are in trouble right now and even you cannot see a way out!" said Tawa.

"No. We protect the Positive Logos and we do not get it involved in the battle. The oath will be honoured," Mogori maintained.

"If we use the Positive Logos, we can find a way to win. But without using the Positive Logos, we're doomed!" Tawa fretted.

"The Positive Logos has ageless and limitless cosmic power. This power is not to be trifled with. Even though the Positive Logos is the positive, pure half of the Logos, that does not mean that it does not have the ability to corrupt and drive whoever wields it to madness. None of us are strong enough to wield the power of the Positive Logos and retain a grip on ourselves. I am not saying any of this to be difficult, Tawa. The power of the Positive Logos could corrupt you to a point where you become worse than the Architect himself if you try to control it," Mogori explained.

"But what if my plan works, Elder Mogori? We could defeat the Mathra for good! From there we could take the Negative Logos from them and destroy the Andromedan armada. With the Positive and Negative Logos in our hands, we could recreate the universe differently. We could create a fair universe; a just universe! Children will go to sleep in peaceful nights with full stomachs. Peoples will live side by side in peace. War, fear, hunger, and hatred will all be a thing of the past!" Tawa extolled.

"It is not our place to decide what the universe is and what it should be!" Mogori yelled. His voice thundered through the cottage and the two could tell that the Pleiadians outside of the cottage fell silent because of the outburst of anger.

Mogori started walking out of the cottage. Tawa watched as Mogori was making his way out. The elder had his back turned to him yet again. Tawa's heart panged with sadness and despair. The Pleiadian could feel his inhibition slipping from him.

"I am going to handle this matter in the best interests of the Pleiadians and in the best interests of the cosmos. I will not force you to comply with my wishes, but I implore you not to interfere," Mogori said as he was walking out.

Tawa let out a scream. Before Mogori could make it to the doorway of the cottage, Tawa released lethal energy beams from his hands that struck Mogori in his back. As the beams shot out and struck Mogori's body, Tawa continued to scream in rage and terror.

As soon as the beams stopped radiating from Tawa's palms, Mogori's body hit the ground as smoke simmered out of the Pleiadian elder's back. Tawa looked down at Mogori's body, horrified at what he had just done to his mentor, elder and friend. Elder Mogori was dead.

Tawa shuddered with guilt and horror. He put his trembling palms to his face and fell to his knees sobbing. Suddenly a wave of resolve came over Tawa and he stopped sobbing immediately. He crawled to Mogori and took the pschent off of his head.

Tawa held the pschent in his clutches, staring at it. He then put the pschent on his own head and stood up. Tawa walked out of the cottage, now looking to take on the position as the new elder of the Pleiadians.

As Tawa stepped out of the cottage, he was met with the Pleiadians in the sanctuary all staring at him. He stood at the doorway looking back at them for a moment. As soon as he realised that he did not have much time, he immediately started walking toward to Positive Logos.

Pleiadian brother, Ozeed, approached Tawa to ask him what had happened in the cottage. "Brother Tawa, is everything okay? We heard the commotion inside of the cottage and were starting to worry," Ozeed inquired.

Tawa kept marching while looking forward, the same way that Mogori beat a path while ignoring him minutes ago. The Pleiadians in the sanctuary began to worry and murmur amongst themselves about what had just happened in the cottage.

Tawa approached the cradle and looked down at the Positive Logos. The Positive Logos was in a peaceful slumber. As he approached the cradle that the Positive Logos was sleeping in, some of the Pleiadians went into the cottage to investigate what happened.

Weeping and wailing could be heard from the inside of the cottage, as some Pleiadians were shocked to learn that their elder had just died. Ozeed began to approach Tawa again, intent on demanding answers.

Tawa immediately grabbed the Positive Logos as his eyes began to give off a blue glow. His body started to glow as the same glow began to surround the body of the Positive Logos as well. Tawa began to scream as the Positive Logos also started crying.

"Tawa, Elder Mogori has died! What happened, brother Tawa? What have you done?" Ozeed asked, on the brink of tears. He marched towards Tawa, but Tawa let off a sonic boom of energy that sent Ozeed and other Pleiadians in the sanctuary flying back.

Tawa began to shake the Positive Logos violently as he held it in his arms. The Positive Logos went from crying to screeching. The glow around Tawa only got brighter and brighter until none of the Pleiadians were able to look on.

The ground of the sanctuary began to shake. Tawa's screams got louder and louder as he felt the life force of the Positive Logos getting absorbed into him. The Positive Logos' visage was beginning to evaporate into the blue glow emanating from Tawa.

The light from Tawa began to flicker as the sonic booms pushed energy outwards, causing gusts that kept the surrounding Pleiadians from approaching him. The light went from flickers to slowly dimming altogether.

Tawa emerged taller than he was before. He had gold patterns all over his purple skin and the face of the Positive Logos was now meshed in his chest. Tawa started to levitate as the other Pleiadians looked on in terror.

Ozeed looked on in rage and terror. The Pleiadian go to his feet and charged at Tawa for an attack. Tawa raised his hand in Ozeed's direction and the Pleiadian immediately combusted into dust. The other Pleiadians screamed in dread.

Tawa levitated higher into the air until all of the Pleiadians in the sanctuary could see him. The Pleiadians fell silent as they looked up at their new leader. Tawa looked down at his brothers with a menacing scowl.

"Pleiadians, all lifeforms and all lovers of peace alike. Rejoice! Your saviour is here. The Mathra will not have the victory on this day. The Architect will not be able to withstand my power. Queen Natiki is a mere insect in my mighty presence!" Tawa declared.

"You are no leader to the Pleiadians!" shouted a defiant Pleiadian in the sanctuary. Tawa turned around and saw a Pleiadian that was much younger than him, standing amongst the trees.

"You were not chosen by a council of your brothers. The fact that you now control the power of the Positive Logos changes nothing! You have no legitimate claim to call yourself our leader! All you are is a usurper and a murderer!" the young Pleiadian shouted.

Tawa looked down at the young Pleiadian with no emotion. The young Pleiadian unleashed an energy beam and sent it flying up in Tawa's direction. As soon as it reached Tawa, he touched the beam of light with his fingertip.

The beam refracted back to the young Pleiadian with multiple times more force and intensity and ended up destroying the very same Pleiadian that it came from. A nearby Pleiadian screamed in horror right afterwards.

"Now that you see what I am capable of, I suggest that you comply with my wishes. You dare to scoff at my offer of salvation? Mogori would have had you fight a losing battle to your deaths before he allowed us to use the power of the Positive Logos to give us a fighting chance against the Pleiadians. How is that the leader that we deserve? Would the council of Pleiadians have chosen to save you in your hour of need? Or would they have fed you to the furnace of martyrdom at the first sign of trouble, just like Mogori? Why this fidelity to tradition? I offer you life. I offer you safety. I also offer you an opportunity for us to become the greatest civilisation in the universe. And that is exactly what I am going to do. With the power of the Positive Logos in my hands, I will destroy the Architect and take the Negative Logos from him. Once I have the power of the unified Logos, I will destroy Queen Natiki and her Andromeda legions. Once I am done with the despots, I will reshape this universe. The cosmos will be awash with resources. All oppressive colonies will be neutralised. Every chain of oppression will be broken and at the summit of it all, I will stand as your king, your lord, and your liberator!" said Tawa.

Pleiadians in the sanctuary began to weep and cry for their departed leader. Tawa looked down on them with silent contempt. A small group of Pleiadians carried Mogori's body out of the cottage as they mourned him.

They carried the dead leader to the tallest tree in the sanctuary and wrapped his body in bands. They set the bands on fire and cremated the beloved leader. Tawa looked down at them with a vacant expression.

156

The Pleiadians continued to sing chants to the heavens in memory of their elder. Tawa turned to his side and spat; arms crossed waiting for the Pleiadians to declare their undying loyalty to him. Instead, the Pleiadians kept on chanting.

"Not to interrupt the sentimental moment, but you people have some important decisions to make, and time is running out!" Tawa yelled. The mourning Pleiadians kept on chanting as though they could not even hear Tawa.

"Enough! You are staring oblivion in the face and all you can do is chant? I am trying to save you from destruction! I will not let you forfeit everything that we have and everything that we could still accomplish!" Tawa yelled.

The Pleiadians turned up and looked at Tawa all at once. Tawa looked back down at the Pleiadians in the sanctuary, as if they would capitulate and acknowledge him as their leader at any moment. Instead, his mourning brothers stared at him.

Soon the Pleiadians' attention shifted to another new detail in the sky. A bright ember dot appeared in the sky and was getting larger with every passing minute. Tawa turned around to look at what just got their attention.

It was clear to everyone in the sanctuary that they were no longer alone. The light in the sky was the Mathra mothership and it had just arrived in the atmosphere of Kappess moon. The commotion turned to grave silence.

The Mathra mothership in the sky appeared as a tiny red sparkly in the sky which got bigger and bigger until it started to take shape. Soon the lobster-shaped space vessel loomed large in the air for all of Kappess moon to see.

The Pleiadians looked up at the Mathra vessel with silent trepidation. A sinister smile broke on Tawa's face, as he realised that his brothers would have to choose between loyalty to him and certain death.

Tawa looked up at the approaching ship and smiled. "I guess your time is up, my Pleiadian brothers. As the hour approaches, so does my age. And what an incredible age it will be! Regardless of whether you are with me or against me, it's finally time to pay the piper," he mused.

Chapter 10: Warriors, Heroes and Kings

Location: Mali Empire, West Africa, circa 1324.

Menzi walked out of the dark, cloudy, ethereal gateway portal that had spirited him to two other time periods before, as he walked into a desert plain that seemed to go on until forever in every direction that he looked.

The sun was at the highest point in the sky and his shadow was a round squatty circle that hid right under his body at this hour. He could tell that it was high noon, and although he was unsure about his exact location, he knew he must have been there to meet the great Mali king, Mansa Musa.

The heat from the midday sun beat down on Menzi's head as he shielded his eyes by placing his palm over his face. As he turned to his side, he saw a caravan of camels, horses, livestock, and soldiers travelling in the north-east direction.

Menzi began to walk in the direction of the caravan, knowing that the travellers were likely to lead him to the person he was there to see. The closer he got as he jogged, the clearer the soldiers, flute players, cooks, priests, and scouts were in his view.

The caravan easily had tens of thousands of people. Menzi could see men holding large golden staffs as they walked in the caravan. Thousands of camels walked amongst them carrying massive bags filled with gold. Menzi was sure he had never seen so much gold in one place.

Menzi took one of the Nommo tablets in his pouch. He immediately began to feel his mind open up and his body temperature start to regulate more acutely. He found the point in the caravan where the carriage that carried the master of the thousands in the caravan was.

As Menzi approached the caravan a wary guard stopped, turned, and motioned for Menzi to keep his distance, hand on his scimitar, ready to draw it out and strike the young Nommo warrior. Menzi stopped in his tracks and raised his hands decorously.

"You will not come any closer," the guard warned dutifully. Other guards soon stopped and began to surround Menzi. The caravan stopped advancing as scouts in the caravan struck their staffs on the ground twice, signalling that the caravan should rest.

A hand swiped the curtain on the imperial carriage open. A man in regal clothing looked out and saw Menzi. He had a wise demeanour to his face and even sitting down, it was clear that he was of great stature. As soon as the man in the carriage saw Menzi he smiled as if he saw a long-lost friend.

The man stepped out of the carriage and walked towards Menzi. "I know well enough that life is full of surprises. But even I did not expect Elder Amma to send me a messenger while I am on my Hajj pilgrimage. This must be important," the man said.

Menzi immediately took to one knee and bowed as a show of respect to the man. However, the man objected. "Please, young man. You are a Nommo warrior. There is no need for you to bother with all of that," the man said, smiling sincerely.

Menzi got back up. Still keeping his head down, he thanked the man. "Thank you, Your Highness. I was sent back here to find King Mansa Musa. I believe that is you?" Menzi asked as he looked up at the man.

"Your scouting skills are most impressive, young Nommo. You have found who you were looking for. I am King Mansa Musa," the man said with a smile while spreading his arms. Menzi looked up at King Mansa and smiled.

Mansa Musa sidestepped to give Menzi a clear view of the carriage he had just walked out of. "Come in. I'm sure that you are here on important business, and we have a lot to discuss. I am on my way to Mecca, but I definitely have time to spare to talk to someone sent by Elder Amma," he said.

Mansa Musa led Menzi into the carriage. The two hopped in and Menzi was amazed by the amount of space in the carriage and the level of comfort it offered for a mode of luxury transportation from the 1300s.

Mansa Musa offered Menzi a cup of water from a pitcher and Menzi politely obliged. As he took a sip, he noticed that the cup and the pitcher were both made of gold. He looked around at the gold trim that covered the curtains, Mansa Musa's clothes and the cushions they sat on.

"I read about you during my history lessons. We are told that you might have been the richest man that has ever lived, even all the way up to the twenty-first century. By the looks of your caravan and your carriage and all of this gold, you certainly are," Menzi remarked.

163

Mansa Musa gave Menzi a wily smile. "That's enough about that. Why has Elder Amma sent you to me?" Mansa Musa asked Menzi. The young Nommo warrior finished with his last gulp of water and put the golden cup he was drinking from aside.

"I wasn't sent by Elder Amma personally. In fact, I've never met the elder before. I was in a Mathra spaceship with the Positive Logos. The Mathra were about to get their hands on the Positive Logos, and I just remember being engulfed by some light that came out of nowhere and before I knew it, I was on a world orbiting the Zeta Reticuli's cosmic brain. When I found them, they told me that Elder Amma instructed them to send the first Nommo that arrives to different timelines to collect items that will help us defeat the Mathra," Menzi explained.

"It sounds like things have taken a serious turn. And you were all by yourself in the Mathra spaceship protecting the Positive Logos?" Mansa Musa asked.

"It wasn't just me. I was with a Nommo warrior named Mogoma. I don't know where he is at the moment or if he is even alive. But when we were trapped in the Mathra spaceship trying to protect the Positive Logos from them, it was just the two of us," said Menzi.

"Ah, yes! Mogoma. He's one of the best that we have. Very gifted warrior indeed," Mansa Musa quipped as he took a sip of water out of his own golden cup.

"Wait. You know Mogoma?" Menzi exclaimed with disbelief.

"Oh, yes, very well. I know many of the Nommo warriors well. We had a good rapport up to the point when I was assigned here on earth. Didn't you know that?" Mansa Musa asked, stunned by Menzi's disbelief.

"Honestly, it was only a few days ago that I realised that I was even a Nommo at all. Before that, I was just an ordinary boy from a city called Durban about to become a university student and none of this was remotely a part of my world," said Menzi.

"That is rather strange, Menzi. There are many Nommo like us throughout history who appear to have lived ordinary or even remarkable human lives. But we always have the knowledge of where we come from and their mission to protect humanity," Mansa Musa said.

"Why is it that the Nommo do that, King Mansa Musa? Why do they send their own to earth? Why do the Nommo care if the people of earth are safe and protected? I mean, from what I have seen, we don't add much value to the universe and the way we live is actually harmful to the very planet that we rely on for our lives," Menzi asked.

"What we do for the people of earth, we do for billions of civilisations across the cosmos. We walk amongst them as invisible guides helping them on their path to cosmic maturity. Trying our best not to intervene or interfere with their growth and development as a people," said Mansa Musa.

"And nobody else knows that you exist? Well, except for the billions of people who witnessed the Mathra invasions in my timeline," Menzi inquired further.

"The Dogon tribe of Mali know us very well. We are central to their spiritual beliefs. They even know all about our home planet Nibiru, in the Sirius star system. Their faith speaks of a powerful fish people who come from the stars and will one day return to save them. Are you following me on this?" Mansa Musa asked.

"Woah...no way...!" Menzi marvelled.

"We have been here for thousands of years, Menzi. Your mentor Mogoma is thousands of years old. That is how I know who he is. Even you, Menzi, will live for thousands of years from this point. And as a Nommo, you have incredible power and wisdom in you. You just don't remember it right now," Mansa Musa said.

"Then why do the Nommo trust me so much with such an important mission if I don't even remember who or what I am?" Menzi asked as a single tear trailed down his face.

"That I do not know, Menzi. But what I do know is that Elder Amma is bound to all of her children by love; love for her children, love for the cosmos and love for peace," Mansa Musa responded.

Mansa Musa reached into his imperial robe and pulled out a large, egg-shaped nugget adorned with strange inscriptions. He took Menzi's hand and placed the nugget into the young Nommo's open palm.

Menzi looked at the nugget. He saw beautiful shapes and images inscribed on its surface. Its golden colour shimmered even in the intimate dim light of Mansa Musa's carriage. Menzi lifted this hand, holding the nugget up so that he could admire its beauty.

"What you are holding in your hand is from the planet Nibiru. It was held by Elder Amma herself. It is one of my most prized possessions, over everything else that I own in the entire Mali empire," Mansa Musa said to Menzi.

"It's beautiful," said Menzi. "But what is it exactly? It looks to me like an elaborately decorated easter egg," Menzi wondered.

"It's a Nommo orb. The inscriptions on the surface tell the story of the universe. The round shape represents the unity of all things, living and non-living, throughout the cosmos. The inscription tells the story of how the smallest parts of the universe collided to create worlds, stars, trees, mountains, fish, birds, beasts, and mankind. That even though we are different and are from different parts of the cosmos, we all come from the same place," Mansa Musa said.

Menzi mouthed "wow" as he continued to look at the detail on the Nommo orb. "And you're giving this to me?" he asked the Mali king. Mansa Musa nodded with a smile. Menzi smiled back at the king and put the Nommo orb in his pouch.

"And what does it do?" Menzi asked Mansa Musa earnestly.

"It has the space and time manipulation capability of the Negative Logos. Whoever wields it, can shape time and space around themselves like a tapestry, momentarily. It's power is not absolute, but for a few seconds, you can hold waterfalls in place, hop between galaxies or move a moon," Mansa Musa said.

"Amazing! Is it as powerful as the Logos?" Menzi asked.

"Definitely not," said Mansa Musa. "The combined Logos is still the most powerful object in the universe. That is why it is critical that you make sure that the Architect does not get his hands on the Positive Logos and combine it with the Negative Logos. If you can, I would advise that you not allow the Andromedans to get their hands on it either," he added.

"King Mansa Musa, do you think we are on the right side of history? From what I understand from this war between the Andromedans and the Mathra, the Mathra are on a retributive crusade. Because the Andromedans oppressed them. It feels like as we take a stand against the Mathra, we are excusing what the Andromedan empire has done. It actually reminds me

169

of the history of my own country. Even during present day, we struggle to agree on whether enough was done to make the evil things that were done in the past right. In fact, a lot of what we condemned in the past is still happening today under a different guise. I guess what I'm asking is, what if the Andromedans are the bad guys that need to be defeated and destroyed?" Menzi asked nervously, careful not to elicit the king's rage.

"That is a very important question, young Nommo. There is no mistaking that the Andromedan Empire has brought hell upon other civilisations around the universe by expanding their dominion across the stars. The Mathra's mission to destroy the universe is an urgent matter and they must be stopped, regardless of whether the Andromedans were right or wrong. But the beauty of surviving this war and winning is that you get to decide what happens next. The hunter no longer needs to tell the story of the lion on the lion's behalf. Maybe that is why it is you that is sitting with me at this moment, young Nommo. Your youth means that you are bold enough to imagine a new cosmos that works differently from what has always worked for ions before you were born. People think gold resolves problems and that wealth makes troubles go away. Sometimes all you need is the imagination and the courage to envision a better world than the one that already exists. And what that new universe looks like is up to you. It is your battle too, young Nommo. If you overcome adversity, you get to decide what it means," Mansa Musa said to the young Nommo warrior.

Menzi nodded as the king spoke. "And what do you think should happen to Andromeda and the Mathra after all of this is over? Should the Mathra get reparations? Should Andromeda become a republic? Are changes like that even possible?" Menzi asked.

"You know better than me, young Nommo. You know better than me," said Mansa Musa. Menzi looked at the king in the eyes and nodded solemnly. Mansa Musa beamed a warm smile back at the young Nommo.

"You should probably get going now," said Mansa Musa.

Menzi sat up and gathered his belongings and prepared to head back to the present day. The Mansa pulled the curtain of the imperial carriage aside and raised his hand outside of the curtain. The two immediately felt the carriage come to a stop.

Two servants opened up the curtain for the king and the young Nommo warrior to come out of the carriage. Mansa Musa and Menzi stepped out of the carriage and embraced. Menzi looked Mansa Musa in the eyes again and smiled.

"Thank you," Menzi beamed. "I came here so unsure of myself and shaken in my confidence. I feel strengthened and supported after meeting and speaking to you. I think I know what I need to do now and I have a lot of faith that this battle can be won," Menzi said.

"Your visit to me has been a blessing, young Nommo. I hope that as you head back home, you do not forget that you are supported by ageless forces. The Nommo are in your corner wherever you are. You will overcome," said Mansa Musa.

The two released each other from the embrace. Menzi turned around and pulled the Nommo herb out of his bag. He went down and one knee and set the herb on fire. As the smoke from the burning herb conjured a portal in front of Menzi, he turned around and gave Mansa Musa one more smile.

Menzi pulled out the egg-shaped nugget and held it up in front of the portal. Streaks of shimmering gold light hopped from the nugget into the portal's vortex. In the heart of the portal the orange skies of the moon orbiting the Zeti Reticuli's cosmic brain were clear.

172

Menzi walked into the portal, heading back to the home of the Zeta Reticuli in present day. The young Nommo warrior knew that on the other side of the portal, he would come face to face with the most important mission he has ever had in his life.

Chapter 11: Planet wars

Location: Kappess Moon, the Pleiades.

Tawa stood still, smiling with anticipation as the Mathra mothership descended on the sanctuary of Kappess Moon, causing a strong gust of wind to blow in all directions. The jets roared as the mothership touched the ground.

Trees bent away from the direction of the ship as the wind blew and the ground trembled slightly as the mothership landed. The Pleiadians that were preparing to fight Tawa for assassinating Mogori moments ago were now focusing on the Mathra mothership.

"This is the time for us to unite against the Mathra, my brothers," Tawa said. "You are to protect the Positive Logos from the Architect. The fate of the universe is depending on us," the newly self-appointed leader of the Pleiadians said.

The young Pleiadian warrior, Ozeed, walked up to Tawa with a sure stride. He looked straight at Tawa with rage in his eyes. Tawa looked back at Ozeed, smirking. "This does not change anything. If we defeat the Mathra, I'm making this right," Ozeed hissed.

"I have every intention of ruling in the best interests of my fellow Pleiadians, Ozeed. You would do well to take a moment to ask yourself for whom you are fighting. Your people or a dead leader with outdated ideas? Take your time...once we've dealt with more immediate emergencies, of course," Tawa said before turning his attention to the now opening Mathra mothership.

The hangar door began to open slowly as smoke began to waft out of the Mathra mothership. As the door opened fully, Mathra carpenters started marching out onto the grounds of the sanctuary. The Pleiadians looked on, some gasping, others trembling.

The Carpenters were tall and imposing, even in comparison to the Pleiadians. They were armed with weapons that released photon blasts and were so large that could only be carried with at least two arms. They exited the mothership and stood in a right angle formation facing the Pleiadians.

After the armed Carpenter foot soldiers got out of the mothership a lone Mathra Welder emerged from their midst. The Welder walked out until he was front and centre of the formation of Carpenters that had just come out of the mothership.

The Welder was much smaller than the Carpenters but had the demeanour of an authority figure. As the Welder assumed its position, Tawa was standing directly in front of it mere meters away. The Welder prostrated itself and prepared to speak.

"Pleiadians, arise and rejoice. Your eyes are about to behold the terror, splendour, and majesty of the lord of the universe in waiting. Savour the privilege of being the last to see him as master of the Mathra and the first to see him as ruler of a new universe; a universe completely remade in his image, for his pleasure and his purpose. On your knees! Bow and grovel at the feet of your new ruler, the master of your destiny, the claimer of your soul, the Architect!" the Welder exclaimed.

"I'm afraid we will not be doing any of that today," Tawa retorted. "We, the Pleiadians, will not roll over and allow the universe that we call home to be destroyed for any reason. Go back into your vessel and tell the Architect that he will receive no hero's parade of flowers here. We are united against his murderous campaign," Tawa said.

The surrounding Pleiadians stood silent as Tawa spoke. Ozeed wanted to protest to Tawa's assumption of power and tell Tawa that he did not speak for all Pleiadians, but Ozeed also understood that the current situation demanded, at least, a show of false united defiance.

"I was not aware that the Pleiadian had a new leader. Your position on this does not strike me as the thinking of a pacifist. The Mathra has no quarrel with you, but we will not be stopped by any defiance from you. If you do not bow to us, you will hand over the Positive Logos," the Welder said.

"I'm glad my words don't strike you as the words of a pacifist. And yes. The Pleiadians are now under new management. If the Architect thinks we will surrender the Positive Logos, go back in that vessel, and tell him that he has a fight on his hands. Better yet, call him out so that I can tell him myself," Tawa said as he began to levitate, and his eyes gave off a glow.

The Welder looked up at Tawa as he levitated higher and higher above the Mathra. The Welder had a serious and menacing scowl on its face as it stared up at Tawa. The Carpenters on either side of the Welder raised their photon guns and aimed them at Tawa.

"You will deeply regret that you said that. I guarantee you that," the Welder warned. "The Architect has waited for ages for this day to finally arrive and he will not be denied by blue and purple-faced pacifist. Carpenters, shoot!" the Welder ordered.

The Mathra Carpenters aimed their weapons skyward and fired photon blasts at Tawa. Instead of ducking to evade the shots of photon energy, Tawa used his Pleiadian telekinetic abilities to lift the pillars on the temple of the Kappess sanctuary and place them in the way of the photon blasts to absorb the impact of their lethal energy.

Ozeed let out a yell and the Pleiadian warrior-monks charged at the Mathra Carpenters. A massive battle between the Mathra and the Pleiadians ensued. The Welder quickly retreated to the mothership as the Carpenters held off the Pleiadians.

In the bedlam of the scrimmage, a Carpenter managed to take a Pleiadian down with a photon blast from its weapon. Another Pleiadian managed to hurl boulders at a Carpenter from a nearby cliff with his telekinetic power.

Meanwhile, Tawa was surrounded by a small group of Mathra Carpenters. The Mathra foot soldiers all attacked him at once. Tawa managed to push them back away from him with the newfound abilities that he got from combining himself with the Positive Logos.

178

The Carpenters tried to attack Tawa again. He stood at the centre of the scene with his arms stretched out. The blue glow from his body got larger and brighter. As he yelled out, the Carpenters surrounding him were instantly vapourised.

Tawa was about to turn his attention to the Mathra mothership, where the Architect was, but he suddenly felt an arm at his shoulder pulling him back. Tawa turned around to see who it was. It was Ozeed.

"You have killed our mentor and that was bad enough. But to tear the pillars of our sacred temple just to protect yourself from the attack of the Mathra is just adding insult to the injury that you have dealt to us today. It's a flagrant disrespect that I cannot allow," Ozeed warned.

"Please stop fighting brothers," said another Pleiadian who was nearby. "We need to protect ourselves from the Mathra and stop them from getting the Positive Logos," the Pleiadian urged his brothers.

"Just in case you didn't get the memo yet, Tawa, I don't answer to any of you anymore!"

Tawa grumbled. He raised his hand until his palm was directly in front of Ozeed's face and emitted energy from the Positive Logos. An invisible shock wave of energy hit Ozeed, and his body was immediately vapourised.

The Pleiadian that witnessed the exchange cried out, horrified that Tawa would kill another one of his own. He fell to his knees before the ashes that used to be Ozeed. Tawa looked down at him with contempt.

"Let that serve as your last warning, brother. You are either with me or you are my enemy. Are you going to follow me into a new age for the Pleiadians or will you keep turning back to a distant and dead past?" Tawa said in a dispassionate ultimatum.

The Pleiadian began to sob as he mourned his brother. He looked up at Tawa with enraged, tearful eyes. "You murderer!" he shouted. The Pleiadian sprang up from his knees to charge at Tawa to attack him.

The now-power-hungry Pleiadian raised his hand in the face of his mourning brother and vapourised him like he did to Ozeed. "Wrong answer," Tawa said casually as he clapped twice, as if to dust off his weapons.

As Tawa turned his attention to the Mathra mothership, the Architect emerged from the inside of the vessel. The Architect kept himself concealed under a long, black, hooded cloak. The fighting stopped immediately as the Architect emerged.

Tawa slowly began to walk in the direction of the Architect. The Architect slowly stepped out until his feet were standing on Pleiadian soil. Tawa stood firm with his palm raised in the Architect's direction, ready to do battle.

"So, this is the final front of defence standing between me and everything that I have worked for," the Architect mused. "A band of pacifist farmer monks? I was expecting this last stretch of the journey to give me a little more resistance," the Architect scoffed.

"I believe you will be surprised to learn just how much things have changed in a very short space of time, Architect. Because if we are talking about what you are in for, resistance is quite the understatement," Tawa said.

The Architect grinned under the hood of his black cloak, his face still completely hidden from Tawa and the rest of the sanctuary. "My Welder has told me that you want to hear this command straight from my mouth, so here I am. Surrender the Positive Logos or pay the price," the Architect said.

Tawa gave off a glow and started levitating until he was some thirty feet above the Architect. The leader of the Mathra did not even raise his head to keep his eyes on the Pleiadian. Tawa raised his palm in the general direction of the Architect, ready to obliterate him.

"The Positive Logos is with me, Architect. If you want to leave this moon with it, I suggest you come and take it from me. But, as I said, if that is what you want to do, you unfortunately have a fight on your hands," Tawa warned.

Tawa's body immediately started flaring with cosmic energy from the Positive Logos. The Architect remained silent for a moment. "You're playing god with a weapon that could destroy you, pathetic fool!" the Architect blurted out.

Tawa scowled back at the Architect with incredulous anger. "Wish granted," the Pleiadian said under his voice. Tawa released a blast of energy powered by the Positive Logos, the same power that allowed him to vaporise Ozeed.

However, instead of striking the Architect and vaporising his body, the energy settled around the Architect, forming a dome around his body until it was completely dissipated. The Architect stood unharmed and unfazed by the attack.

Tawa looked on, stunned by what he was seeing. The same power he used to turn his brothers into pillars of dust had no visible effect on the Architect. "How? This is impossible. No one should be able to survive that!" the Pleiadian stammered.

"Whatever it is that you have been planning to do, you could not have spent much time thinking it through. That was your first mistake. But don't worry. You won't live long enough to regret it in any event," the Architect warned.

The Mathra leader flung the black cloak off of his body to reveal himself. His humanoid-serpentine form stood firm as he was now staring up at Tawa. He had large beady insectoid eyes, green scales, claws, and sharp teeth.

The Architect also had a large tail whose trunk was as large as his torso. On the left side of the Architect's abdomen, sat what appeared to be a growth or tumour which gave off a bright red glow, thumped like a pounding heart, and occasionally undulated.

"Time for the big reveal! You thought you had secured yourself a major advantage because you bonded yourself with the Positive Logos? Well, I have bonded myself with the Negative Logos. My energy has the power to cancel your attacks out. That's right. Like a kiss from an angel in the dark, I didn't even feel it," the Architect gloated.

Tawa gulped, realising that the power he had just attained was not enough to guarantee him a victory over the Architect and the Mathra. His mind recalled the warning that Mogori gave him in the last moments of his life.

"No! I will not let you defeat me! I won't lose! I refuse to lose!" Tawa yelled. The Pleiadian swooped down, charging at the Architect for an attack. As Tawa got within swiping distance right above the Architect, the leader of the Mathra raised his hands, telepathically keeping Tawa suspended in air.

Tawa gasped with shock as he had just lost control over his own body's movements. The Architect gave him a sadistic smile and sprang forth, striking the Pleiadian with a mean headbutt and sending him

184

flying back some five hundred meters. Tawa's body rammed against rock solid boulders.

The Architect slowly walked towards Tawa, stalking the Pleiadian for sport. Tawa writhed in pain as he pulled himself up until he was on his feet again. "I'm surprisingly glad you didn't surrender the Positive Logos. This is actually a lot more fun," the Architect taunted.

"I'll show you fun in just a second," Tawa strained as his legs buckled momentarily. The Pleiadian let out another sudden blast from the powers of the Positive Logos directly in front of the Architect's face, with a massive, bright, blue beam shooting directly at the Mathra leader's face.

Instead of reacting in any way to the shot, the Architect reached for Tawa's arm, grabbed it, and twisted it violently. As Tawa's body shifted with the Architect's twists, he lost his balance. The Architect sprang up off of his feet, balanced on his tail and delivered a dropkick to Tawa.

Tawa's body flew back to where the now collapsed temple of the sanctuary was. As soon as Tawa hit the ground, he scrambled to stagger back up to his feet. He looked around at the bricks and pillars that once formed the temple.

This time he used his Pleiadian abilities to lift every boulder and rock he could see telekinetically, as the Architect slowly approached him. The rocks and boulders began to rise as they were surrounded by a blue glow that was similar to the one that surrounded Tawa's body.

Instantly, a barrage of rocks and boulders went flying in the direction of the Architect and pummelled him. However, as soon as the rocks and boulders covered the Architect, the leader of the Mathra pushed them off of his body and sent them flying in all directions.

Tawa gave off a blue Pleiadian glow, causing the boulders that flew in his direction to phase right through him. He looked on at the Architect with dread in his eyes, at a loss for how he was to defeat his adversary.

Some of the boulders flew at the fighting Mathra Carpenters and Pleiadians, striking some with maximum impact while Pleiadians who saw them coming fast enough allowed the boulders to phase through them. The Architect emerged with an enraged look on his face. He looked directly at Tawa.

"Alright. I have changed my mind. The fun and games are over. I refuse to waste another second of my time with these games. Surrender the Positive Logos to me. Now!" demanded the Architect, irritated by Tawa's defiance.

Tawa stood defiant and drew in a deep breath before responding. "Firstly, I would rather have you pull the Positive Logos out of my cold, dead corpse than surrender it to you. And secondly, it looks like I am the least of your worries now because we have company," the Pleiadian said.

Tawa turned to his right and looked into the distant horizon. The Architect's attention followed in the direction Tawa's gaze shifted towards. The two looked on as two bright lights appeared in the sky. They both knew that these were Andromedan space vessels.

"You didn't tell me that you were bringing guests along, Architect. Although, I don't imagine that they're coming for me. No, if I were into betting, I would wager that they're coming after you," Tawa taunted.

"SILENCE!" the Architect growled, swiping in Tawa's direction and sending an energy wave that struck the

Pleiadian and sent him flying back. The Architect looked out into the distance with rage and worry.

"I am too close to accomplishing my mission now! I will not let anyone stop me. Not this puny Pleiadian, not the Andromedans, nobody!" the Architect yelled out. He raised his arms and began to summon the powers of the Negative Logos while he looked out at the descending vessels.

The Negative Logos attached to the Architect's left abdomen began to glow red and squirm. The Architect sucked his teeth with discomfort, stilling keeping his hands in the air. Suddenly his whole body was surrounded by a red glow and the two distant vessels also had a red glow around them.

The Architect let out an agonising scream as he swung his arms downward. Immediately the two vessels that were descending from the skies accelerated in speed until they were shooting down from the sky like meteors.

The Mathra and the Pleiadians alike looked on as the two vessels fell to the ground and crashed. The Architect panted frantically, struggling to catch his breath after such a mighty feat. He then turned his attention to Tawa.

"Two Andromedan princesses out of the way," the Architect panted to himself with relief. He turned his attention to a wounded Tawa and slowly started walking towards the Pleiadian. "Now I finish this. I cannot stand to be apart from the Positive Logos any longer."

Chapter 12: Return

Location: The cosmic brain, near the radio lobe of a black hole, somewhere in the universe. Present day.

A small cluster of flashing clouds began to gather somewhere on the surface of the Zeta Reticuli's cosmic brain. The clouds formed a gateway out of thin air that opened up from another place in the universe in a completely different time.

Menzi walked out of the portal, having just concluded his visit to the king of the Mali Empire, Mansa Musa. The portal closed behind him. Menzi could see the planet he was teleported to by the Positive Logos on the horizon.

He looked up and around himself, realising that he was on the surface of the cosmic brain, which housed the robotic avatars of the Zeta Reticuli and the computer that generated their simulated universe.

He called to mind the last time that he saw the cosmic brain from a distance. It was the size of a small planet or a moon. The cosmic brain was made of white and grey synthetic materials and had the look of a created object rather than a naturally occurring cosmic object.

It had a massive calyx-like object in its northern hemisphere that served as a passage to get to its centre where the Zeta Reticuli's robotic avatars and the central computer of the cosmic brain could be found.

Menzi wondered to himself what happened to the Zeta Reticuli in their distant past for the advanced alien race to decide that it was best that they turn their back on the real universe and retreat into a computer simulation.

It did not make sense to him that the advanced alien race had seen the entire expanse of the universe then simply decided that there was nothing else worth exploring and retreated into a world they created for themselves, only to come out to conduct repairs to their giant supercomputer.

But Menzi had no time to ponder the philosophical workings behind the decisions of an alien civilisation that was wiser than he could ever imagine. He leapt off of his feet and proceeded to fly into the opening which led to the central computer of the cosmic brain.

He flew into the opening and descended down a tunnel that was 30 kilometres in circumference with lighting throughout the descent. Massive motion-sensitive lights flashed on as he passed by multiple sections of the tunnel and followed his movements.

He saw the core of the cosmic brain getting closer to his view the further he descended. When he finally landed, he was in an all-white room with wall-to-wall monitors. Some monitors displayed sections of the cosmic brain that Menzi had already seen on his way in.

Other monitors showed images and footage of a beautiful world in an advanced civilisation that he assumed was the simulated world inside of the supercomputer. Every Zeta Reticuli uploaded their conscience onto the supercomputer eons ago.

When the Zeta Reticuli built the supercomputer, they also built robot avatars which they used when they needed to repair the cosmic brain or protect it from intruders. Other than that, they lived in a computer simulation where no one went hungry or lacked any resources.

Menzi walked up to the central unit of the supercomputer, where the largest monitor of them all was. He looked at the monitor running immense amounts of code which Menzi had never seen before and could not hope to decipher. It was time to summon the Zeta Reticuli.

"Hello, Sheh! I have returned from my journey. I am back and I am ready to face the Mathra and defeat them once and for all. However, I am going to need some help from you and the rest of the Zeta Reticuli," Menzi called out.

Menzi stood in awkward stillness, almost feeling foolish as he did not even know if calling Sheh out loud would work. He looked around to see if Sheh was outside of the simulation and he perhaps did not notice.

Suddenly the lights in the room dimmed significantly. The supercomputer began to hum with a rising pitch. The room shook slightly. Menzi took a few cautious steps back, unsure of what to expect next. The eyes on a robot avatar sitting nearby lit up.

The humanoid machine stood up and walked up to Menzi. Menzi faced the humanoid machine, waiting to see if it was the same Zeta Reticuli that he spoke to before traveling back to the past. The machine extended its arm out to Menzi.

"Welcome back, Menzi. Congratulations. You made it back alive. Elder Amma's faith in her children was not misplaced. I assume you have a plan to save us all now that you're back," Sheh said to the young Nommo warrior.

"Thank you for the kind words. I believe I have a plan. I don't know if it's guaranteed to work or anything, but if it does, we should be able to stop the Architect for good. But I need your help and I need you to trust me with something very important," Menzi said.

"Certainly, young Nommo. We are committed to helping you however we can. It does sound like you are about to ask a lot of us, but at this point, if the Architect wins, we are all doomed without exception. So, anything you need from us is yours. How can we help?" Sheh asked.

"First, I need you to explain something to me about this cosmic brain. Am I correct in saying that any sentient lifeform can be sat down in those chairs with those contraptions and their consciousness will be uploaded onto the supercomputer?" asked Menzi.

"Yes. It would have to be a sentient being with a certain level of intelligence, but if any being is strapped up to that from this universe, its consciousness will be uploaded onto the supercomputer, where the conscience of every Zeta Reticuli is," Sheh said.

"And once the consciousness is there, in the supercomputer, is it automatically in the simulation? Would it be able to cause havoc in the simulated world of the Zeta Reticuli? Is there any way that it can escape?" Menzi inquired.

"Ha," Sheh uttered, slightly bemused. "Well, the consciousness could escape if its body is still connected to the machinery. It would not be able to immediately access the simulation. We have plenty of safeguards to decide what happens to any uploaded consciousness," Sheh explained.

"And just out of interest's sake, what could the Zeta Reticuli in the simulation do to an unwanted consciousness if they encountered one in the supercomputer?" Menzi asked, now rubbing his chin with intrigue.

"Well, this is not something we have ever had to do, but if a consciousness that is unwelcome is found by the Zeta Reticuli in the supercomputer, it could easily be deleted," Sheh explained.

Menzi smiled at Sheh's machine avatar. He turned around and stood at the end of the tunnel leading out of the control room. "Might I ask you what exactly it is that you are planning, young Nommo?" Sheh asked.

"I am going to need to use the cosmic brain to defeat the Architect. How long can the cosmic brain continue running if it's taken away from the black hole that powers it?" Menzi asked as he turned back to Sheh.

Sheh's head tilted. "Again, this is not something that the Zeta Reticuli has ever had to do before. But there is an energy reserve mechanism that could allow the cosmic brain to keep the simulation and everything else that the brain does running for sixty earth minutes," Sheh responded.

"Wonderful. If my plan works, I definitely don't think I will need an earth hour to get it done. It's just like some last-minute high school homework. It's all about momentum and timing and if we can get that right, we can beat the Architect. Do you trust me?" Menzi asked Sheh.

"I have to admit, the more I hear of this strategy of yours, the more it sounds like a gamble than a plan. However, the stakes are as high as ever. Our intelligence tells us that both the Negative and the

Positive Logos are on Kappess Moon in the Pleiades. You are our last hope," Sheh said.

Menzi's face turned serious for a moment. He looked down and brooded as it dawned on him how close the Architect probably was to fulfilling the accomplishment of his mission. He looked at Sheh's robotic avatar and nodded dutifully.

"I understand. I hope you know that I would not ask to do this if I was not sure that it would have a chance of working. I promise you that I will not let anything happen to the cosmic brain. It will be back here where it belongs within an hour. I won't let you down," Menzi said.

Sheh nodded back at Menzi and retreated back to the main monitor for his consciousness to return back to the simulation. Menzi took off and flew back up the tunnel until he was back on the surface of the cosmic brain.

Menzi planted his feet on the ground of the cosmic brain's surface. He pulled the egg-shaped nugget that Mansa Musa gave him out of his pouch. He went down on one knee and placed the Nommo herb on the ground and set it on fire.

The smoke from the burning Nommo herb rose until it was in the orbit of the cosmic brain. He placed the nugget in the flames devouring the herb. Ethereal strings of gold sprang from the fire and flew out to the skies.

Menzi looked up to the skies and saw the clouds from the Nommo portals he had become accustomed to using in the sky. This time, there were so many clouds that they covered up the horizon completely.

At the heart of the cloud formation, Menzi could see a pristine light blue sphere and a starry expanse. The cosmic brain slowly began moving into the portal and emerging into another faraway part of the universe.

"Nommo ancestors and guides, empower me!" Menzi called out. "Fortify my steps, direct my path and stay with me. Lift me up and take me to the Pleiades!" Menzi shouted as his eyes gave off a golden glow.

Location: Kappess Moon, the Pleiades.

The Architect stalked Tawa as the Pleiadian was slumped over, lying amongst a pile of rubble. Tawa groaned as he struggled to get back on two feet. He looked into the Architect's black, beady soulless eyes, wondering what he could do to avoid or allay the inevitable.

"You have two choices, Pleiadian. You can either give me what I want, or I can force you to give me what I want. Trust me, you would be much better off if you chose the former," the Architect demanded.

Tawa staggered his way to his feet, still looking at the Architect, his stance showing intentions of defiance. Tawa began to glow, and the power of the Positive Logos started to heal his wounds. The Pleiadian raised his fists, looking straight at the Architect.

"Let's see what else you've got, Mathra. I have plans for the Logos too. However, unlike your plans of utter destruction, I look to expand the resources of the universe so that no one ever knows strife and starvation ever again. I hope to save what you look to destroy," Tawa extolled.

The Architect looked back at Tawa, breathing deeply. "You're kidding yourself, Pleiadian. You think you are the hero between us? This universe is bereft of heroes! That is why I need to grind it down until nothing is left," the Architect.

"Nothing except for you, of course," Tawa retorted. "How very convenient for you. My plan is not to destroy but to save. If I cannot succeed, we say goodbye to our last hope of having a prosperous universe where everyone is equal," said Tawa.

"A prosperous universe where everyone is equal with you as their supreme ruler, of course," the Architect quipped. "You think I am a villain and that you are a saviour, but you've fast lost sight of the reality that the power of the Positive Logos is corrupting you," he taunted.

"Enough!" Tawa lashed out. "You don't get to tell me that I am wrong in this! You are trying to destroy everything the souls of the cosmos hold dear. I am trying to save it from death and hunger. I'm trying to save it from you!" Tawa argued.

"You think you are saving them. But part of you knows that you are power-mad as we speak. I saw the corpses as soon as I arrived in this sanctuary. Do you honestly think I believe those Pleiadians died of old age?" the Architect asked rhetorically.

"Shut up!" Tawa yelled. The Pleiadian sprang up and flew at the Architect for an attack.

Tawa flew at the Architect throwing a mighty right punch. The Architect blocked the punch with his left forearm and swiped at him with a scratch from his right hand. Tawa ducked swiftly and struck the Architect with a flurry of successive punches.

The Architect fell back and landed on the ruins of the now dilapidated sanctuary. Before the Architect could get back to his feet, Tawa flew at him with a mean kick to the face. The Architect writhed in pain as his head swung back and he hit the ground for a second time.

Tawa stood upright and tapped further into the power of the Positive Logos. The Pleiadian gave off a blue glow as the energy from inside of Tawa blew invisible but powerful shock waves in all directions around him. The Architect, still lying on his back, turned, and looked at Tawa, enraged.

"I am well past the point of trying to reason with you or anyone else, Architect. I know what I need to do, and I will not allow you to stop me. I know what needs to be done. No more wasting time. This ends now," Tawa said.

Tawa raised his fists in a combative stance and a pair of massive blades appeared on either of his forearms.

He looked at the Architect in the eyes with a mean scowl. The Architect strained to get back up and evade the coming attack, but his injuries would not allow him.

Tawa jumped forward to launch his fatal attack on the Architect. Suddenly as the Pleiadian made his move, a photon blast came from the periphery and struck Tawa, sending him flying back and landing on his back.

The Architect looked on, still on his back, relieved and astonished. He looked around to see if the Pleiadian was neutralised by a friend or a foe. As the Architect scrambled to get back on his feet, he heard a voice from nearby.

"Servants, one and all! Down your weapons! The newly crown Queen of Andromeda compels you," the voice shrieked. The Architect turned his head and gasped as he saw a towering figure standing at the entrance of the sanctuary. It was the Andromedan royal Natiki, holding a photon rifle.

Natiki's militia ran to the battlegrounds and joined the scrimmage between the Pleiadians and the Mathra Carpenters. Natiki began walking towards the

202

Architect. Tawa lay on the ground, struggling to recover from the photon blast he just took.

"Princess Natiki!" the Architect exclaimed. The leader of the Mathra pushed himself up to a vertical base, knowing that time was no longer on his side. Natiki turned to the Architect and smiled before taking aim at him.

"I am Queen Natiki!" she exclaimed with rage. Natiki let off a photon blast from her weapon. The Architect immediately sprang up. His body gave off a red glowing aura as he hovered in mid-air. The Mathra leader opened his mouth, from which came a lethal, red energy blast. Natiki jumped out of the way of the blast.

The agile Natiki landed gracefully on her feet, only taking her eyes off of the Architect for a split second. She aimed her weapon at the Architect again. "Nobody destroys my spaceship and walks away without suffering the consequences!" she seethed, aiming her weapon at the Architect again.

The Architect was now standing upright, nursing the Negative Logos on the left side of his abdomen with his right hand. The Negative Logos glowed and squirmed as the Architect sucked his teeth in agony. Natiki smiled at the leader of the Mathra as she had an epiphany.

"It's killing you. The energy from the Negative Logos is eating away at your body. If you don't get the Positive Logos soon enough, you will eventually die from the agony. Makes me wonder why you chose to surgically bond it to your body," Natiki said to the Architect.

The Architect gnashed his fangs. "It was to keep it from being taken by the likes of you! I would have rather had it pulled out of my cold, dead corpse than have it stolen by you, like your people have stolen everything else you've ever had! You won't take it from me alive," the Architect said.

"There's more than one way to skin a corpse," Natiki said. She raised her right fist and a massive blade emerged from her armour there. The self-proclaimed Andromedan queen charged at the Architect.

The Architect let out a scream and phased out of sight. Natiki immediately stopped when she saw that the Architect had vanished. Before she knew it, she was surrounded by what looked like scores of identical visages of the Architect standing on the ground and hovering in the air.

Natiki began firing her photon rifle in different directions in an attempt to shoot down all of the Architects that suddenly surrounded her. However, the photon blasts she fired phased right through all the visages she could see, making no visible impact on any of them.

Suddenly the Architect swooped down on Natiki from behind with a powerful roundhouse kick which connected with the Andromedan's neck. The other visages of the Architect disappeared as the leader of the Mathra attacked Natiki with a barrage of punches to the head.

When the Architect was satisfied that he had neutralised Natiki, he stood up over her and opened his palm, ready to vaporise her out of existence. Suddenly, Tawa charged at the Architect from the side and tackled him.

As the Architect and Tawa scrambled on the ground, Natiki got back up and saw her opportunity to kill both the leader of the Mathra and the Pleiadian to claim both the Positive Logos and the Negative Logos for herself. Suddenly she heard a familiar voice in the distance calling her name.

"NATIKI!" the voice shouted. Natiki turned around and saw Princess Innozia riding on an air rover arriving at the Pleiadian sanctuary. "No...no, not now," Natiki fretted to herself as she saw her sister approaching.

"You should have killed me when you had the chance, sister. Surrender now. I am going to take the Positive Logos and the Negative Logos back to planet Nibiru, where they will be taken care off by the Nommo," said the princess as she pulled out a photon rifle of her own.

"Sister. I would advise that you turn around and walk away from this immediately and I just might spare you. If you insist on trying to interfere, you will regret following me to this world," Natiki said to her sister.

Innozia charged her hover rover in Natiki's direction at full speed. Natiki began letting off photon blasts from her rifle. Innozia's peerless reflexes allowed her to jump off of the hover rover and swoop down on Natiki from above with a swift punch.

The two royal Andromedan sisters began to trade blows. Meanwhile, Tawa had managed to overpower the Architect and had him in a headlock. The Pleiadian looked up and saw his brother, Taheeq.

Walking into the battle scene Taheeq looked back at Tawa.

"Brother," Taheeq said. "I am so sorry that we came too late. The sanctuary is in ruins. I can't feel the lifeforce of Father Mogori and brother Ozeed anymore," a devastated Taheeq said to Tawa. Taheeq's attention shifted to the Architect's attention as Tawa choked him.

"As much as I wish I could take the credit for taking these lives of these Pleiadians," the Architect explained "The destruction of the sanctuary and these killings were not my doing. If you want to know who is responsible, ask your brother who strangles me," the Architect strained to say.

Taheeq took a step back, stunned by what the Architect was implying. "What is he talking about, brother Tawa," Taheeq asked. Tawa shoved the Architect aside and turned to Taheeq. "Taheeq, I can explain," he said. Tawa began walking towards Taheeq.

"Tawa, what did you do? Where are our brothers? What happened to them?" Taheeq asked. "You look different. The power from within you; it's so great and terrifying. What did you do, Taheeq? What did you do?!" Taheeq demanded to know.

Tawa began slowly and silently walking towards Taheeq, showing absolutely no emotion. Taheeq prepared for a fight, was still astonished at his fellow Pleiadian's strange behaviour. "I'm sorry, Taheeq. I had to do it," the Pleiadian said as he raised his hand in Taheeq's direction.

Taheeq let out an enraged cry as he flew in Tawa's direction and punched him in the face. Taheeq hit Tawa with a combination of punches while the Architect got his strength back up. Innozia's militia came to the aid of the Pleiadians, fighting the Mathra and Natiki's soldiers.

"You killed our family, Tawa! Why?!" Taheeq demanded as he continued to strike Tawa, who was trying to use his arms to parry away the attack. Taheeq stood up over Tawa and used his telekinetic power to raise a wall from the now-destroyed temple of the Pleiadian sanctuary.

Tawa looked up and saw the wall levitating behind Taheeq. Tawa raised his hand reluctantly, ready to vaporise his brother. He released the power of the Positive Logos through his palm and aimed it directly at Taheeq. Suddenly the Architect shoved Taheeq aside and absorbed Tawa's shot.

The power of the Negative Logos allowed the Architect to absorb and neutralise the blast that Tawa let off through the Positive Logos. The Architect immediately dug his claws into Tawa's torso and pulled them in opposite directions. Tawa's stomach burst open, as the Pleiadian cried out.

The Architect dug through Tawa's entrails and pulled out what looked like a baby covered in blood and flesh. It was the Positive Logos. Mid-fight with her sister Natiki, Innozia caught sight of this moment and tried to run to the Architect to stop him.

The Architect held the shrieking baby in his arms and proceeded to swallow the baby whole. Natiki tackled Innozia, trying to stop her from seizing the Logos and the two sisters continued to tussle as the Architect closed in on accomplishing his mission. It was done.

The Architect was beginning to fuse his own body with that of the Positive Logos, as the leader of the Mathra let out a maniacal laugh. Taheeq screamed as he crawled in the direction of the Architect in vain. Innozia managed to fight Natiki off, but realised she was too late to stop the Architect.

The ground of Kappess moon started to shake uncontrollably as the once red glow that surrounded the Architect now turned purple. The Architect convulsed as the power of both the Positive and negative Logos coursed through his body.

"What's happening?" Innozia said. Taheeq and the Andromedan princess looked on in despair. "He did it. He accomplished his mission. He is combining the Positive Logos and the Negative Logos. We have failed," Taheeq said gravely.

The Architect got larger in size and became more fiendish in his appearance. Innozia's soldiers, Natiki's militia, the Pleiadians and the Mathra Carpenters looked on in awe and horror. The sanctuary fell silent.

Everyone looked on, expecting the Architect to speak. Instead, the Architect looked up. A huge shadow came down on the sanctuary on Kappess. Everyone else's eyes were fixed on the Architect, even though the leader of the Mathra was looking upward. "He's here," the Architect said.

Everyone was now turning up and looking to the sky. There was a mysterious eclipse that turned the sanctuary dark as an unknown object got in the way of the star that Kappess got its light from. The Architect abruptly jumped up and flew to the skies.

Innozia looked up, still confused. "Where is he going?" She asked. Mogoma looked up with her. His Nommo inclination gave him an explanation as to why the star in the sky was being blocked suddenly. "It's Menzi. Menzi is up there. I can feel him!" Mogoma exclaimed.

Location: in orbit of Kappess moon

Menzi stood on the surface of the Zeta Reticuli cosmic brain, as the dark clouds that surrounded the supercomputer disappeared and gave way for the stunning light blue atmosphere of the moon of Kappess in the Pleiades.

He looked down at the moon and could feel the lifeforce of the Architect barrelling upward in his direction. This was the moment of truth. There was no more time for preparation for the young man from Durban. Menzi jumped off of the cosmic brain and began descending rapidly to Kappess.

Menzi and the Architect resembled two comets on a collision course from a distance as they flew closer and closer to each other. The further Menzi went, the clearer the Architect appeared to him in all of his grotesque and fiendish horror.

Menzi pulled out the pipe instrument that Mogoma gave him in the lagoon and blew into it. Sure enough, it successfully summoned the Mazomba. The giant anthropomorphic sea monster emerged amid the battle between the Pleiadians, the Andromedans and the Mathra, towering over everyone in the battlefield.

The two were finally in eyeshot of one another. Menzi swiftly raised his fist and landed a clean punch in the Architect's face. The two were now descending rapidly back to the ground as they furiously grappled and traded hits.

The hard ground of Kappess drew closer and closer the more that Menzi and the Architect tussled. The Architect grabbed Menzi and turned the trajectory of his own fall around so that Menzi would hit the ground first and break the Architect's fall.

Still in freefall, Menzi managed to pull the golden nugget he received from Mansa Musa out of one of his pouches and held it up. A portal suddenly appeared on the ground where he and the Architect would land and instead of hitting the ground, the two disappeared into the portal.

A portal appeared amongst the Andromedan soldiers, the Mathra and the Pleiadians and Menzi and the Architect violently tumbled out of it. Menzi managed to find his footing and stood in a combative stance, ready to face the Architect.

In contrast, the Architect stumbled out of the portal and was disoriented. They were surrounded by Taheeq, Innozia, Natiki, and Mogoma as Menzi stood at the ready to fight the leader of the Mathra. The Architect got back to his feet and roared at everyone surrounding him.

The five warriors attacked the Architect all at once, knowing that he could not be allowed to use the newly combined Logos to wipe out all life in the universe. They clobbered at the Architect, who hid his head under his arms.

The gigantic Mazomba tore through the Mathra and the Natiki's militia, giving the heroes a significant advantage in the broader battle, while a select few fought hard to bring the Architect to submission.

Suddenly the Architect thrusted outward, sending the five flying back almost effortlessly. "Enough of these games!" the Architect exclaimed. "I am so close to getting everything I have hoped for. I will not let you stop me!"

Menzi ran directly at the Architect, but the leader of the Mathra slapped him out of the way. Natiki immediately attacked the Architect from behind. The Architect turned around just in time and grabbed Natiki by her neck. Shock waves ran through Natiki's body as she stood paralysed.

The Architect swiftly lifted Natiki off of the ground. Her skin peeled off completely as her body left the ground as she screamed. The others looked on horrified. Natiki struggled to get out of the Architect's grip while her raw flesh was completely exposed.

Still choking Natiki with one hand, the Architect let out a growl and the Andromedan princess turned to stone immediately. He violently threw the remains of Natiki with a force that broke her now-stone body into thousands of little pieces.

Menzi knew that it was the perfect time to strike. The young Nommo warrior pounced on the Architect with the golden nugget in his clenched right fist. However, instead of delivering a punch that connected with the Architect's body, Menzi punched into a portal he conjured on the Architect's back.

The Architect squirmed in pain. He tried to reach behind him to grab Menzi, but Innozia leaped forward and subdued one of the Architect's arms. Mogoma came to assist and Taheeq held the Architect's other arm.

Menzi reached his other arm into the portal. The young Nommo screamed as he started to pull with all of his strength. Soon it became clear that Menzi was pulling a baby out of the portal. It was the Positive Logos. The baby screamed as Menzi tried desperately to pull it out of the portal.

The Architect's agony intensified as he screamed even louder. Even though the Architect was in pain, the warriors did not feel his strength diminishing as they tried to subdue him. Menzi eventually fell on his back with the Positive Logos out of the Architect's body and in Menzi's arms.

"I have a plan. I need you all to hold the Mathra and Natiki's militia off. I need the Architect to follow me for this to work," Menzi said to Innozia and the others. They looked to each other confused about what Menzi said. Innozia looked at Menzi, unflinchingly, and nodded in approval.

Menzi ran in the opposite direction and immediately took flight, the Positive Logos still in the tight grip of his arms. The Architect reduced in size, skill screaming. The others stepped back from the leader of the Mathra.

Sure enough, the Architect decided to chase after Menzi, hoping to get the Positive Logos back. The Architect flew away and Menzi's allies looked, hoping that the young Nommo's plan would work, whatever it was.

Menzi turned around as he flew towards the Zeta Reticuli cosmic brain and could see the Architect furiously flying behind him, giving chase. Menzi gulped and opted to look straight ahead. The further he flew the darker the sky got.

Innozia proceeded to give order to her militia to cooperate with the Pleiadians under Taheeq's instructions. Her attention immediately turned to the militia from Andromeda that was led by her sister Natiki.

"Andromedans. Natiki has fallen in battle. You are now given the option to join my militia under a united Andromedan army, as our campaign to defeat the Mathra and secure the safe recovery of the Logos continues. Those who mutiny will be tried for treason by Andromeda," she announced to all Andromedan soldiers on the battlefield.

Meanwhile, Menzi finally arrived at the cosmic brain and flew down the tunnel that led to the supercomputer that controlled the cosmic brain. Menzi turned around to look behind him and, sure enough, the Architect was still behind him.

He finally landed in the control room. He quickly placed the Positive Logos down and used the gold nugget to create another portal. He picked up the Positive Logos and gently placed it inside the portal before closing the portal up again.

Menzi turned around, ready to face the Architect. The cosmic brain began to shake violently as the Architect got closer to the control room. Menzi stiffened his face, determined not to allow himself to be consumed by fear.

The Architect landed with a violent stomp. Menzi stood right in front of him. The young Nommo warrior expected the Architect to be livid with him for stealing the Positive Logos from him after he had successfully seized it.

"That will be the last time that you ever try to foil me plans, puny fish man. I will make sure that you pay with your life for your churlish defiance!" the Architect seethed.

"I am not afraid anymore. You can turn away right now and surrender and all will be forgiven. But if you choose to fight me now, I will have no other choice than to destroy you. I cannot allow you to destroy this universe," Menzi warned.

The Architect let out a sinister giggle. The giggle got louder and louder until it was a disdainful guffaw. Menzi slightly adjusted his feet as he fought the urge to flee, opting rather to stand his ground and fight.

"You are foolish for aligning yourself with the Andromedans," the Architect said. "Do you know what they did to my home planet; the enslavement, the oppression, the torture, the dehumanisation, and continued marginalisation that my people have suffered at their behest and at their pleasure? They look at us like monsters, but no. They are the brutes! You know it too! You have seen peoples get oppressed and treated unjustly in your short life. I feel the anger it causes you, coursing through your veins. You know I am right," the Architect told Menzi.

"I know about oppressors myself. I also know about liberators who fought oppressors not to free their own people, but to replace the oppressors that their people lived under in the first place. Tyranny has many faces. It comes out of many corners of existence. We are compelled to fight against that tyranny, but more than anything else, we must fight to make sure that the hate we have for that tyranny does not consume us and make us like those who dehumanise us. If we allow it to consume us, the people we swear to liberate and serve will be burnt down by our own hate, as we insist that we are liberating them," Menzi responded.

"You're a fool," the Architect huffed. "Enough of these platitudes. Give me the Positive Logos immediately!" the Architect demanded, reaching his hand out until it was right in front of Menzi's face.

Menzi stepped back and raised his fists. The Architect tilted his head in curious confusion. Menzi looked at the Architect in his cold soulless eyes. "You want the Positive Logos? You're just going to have to take it from me," Menzi said defiantly.

The Architect roared and swiped at Menzi. The young Nommo warrior ducked and began to run away from the Architect. Menzi ducked successive swipes from the Architect as he retreated. The leader of the Mathra followed Menzi through the maze of the control room.

As his frustration grew, the Architect began to fire sonic beams at Menzi. The Nommo ducked the beams as they exploded on different surfaces of the cosmic brain's control room. Menzi started to make his way to another section of the control room.

This part of the control room in the cosmic brain was darker than the parts of the control room Menzi had just moved from. The surroundings went quiet suddenly and Menzi looked around as he slowly tip-toed around, prepared for the Architect to attack him from any side at all.

Menzi shook as he drew a Nommo blade out from his armour. He looked over both shoulders as his breathing trembled. As he looked up, he saw the Architect scaling the ceiling of the dark section of the control room. The Architect pounced. Menzi tried to retreat but was backed into a corner.

"Now I've got you," the Architect hissed. Menzi looked up at the Architect and tried to stop himself from shaking. "I gave you your chance to obey and you chose to give me this foolish run around. Now I am happy to pull the Positive Logos from your cold dead hands," the Architect demanded.

Menzi raised the arm which carried his Nommo blade higher, as he hid his other hand behind his back. The Nommo parted his feet on the floor, showing that he was ready to defend the Positive Logos with one last fight.

"Very well," the Architect acquiesced. Suddenly a portal appeared right behind Menzi, and he jumped backwards into it. The Architect reached out to grab Menzi and stop him from vanishing, but the portal immediately closed up and he was too late.

A portal suddenly opened up behind the Architect. Menzi came leaping out of the portal with his blade raised above his head. With a clean sweep, Menzi dealt a cut to the Architect's left side. The Architect cried out in agony. Menzi had just cut the Negative Logos off of the Architect's body.

The Architect's wound gushed green slime all over the control room as the Mathra leader shrank even further and took on a form that was halfway reptilian and halfway insectoid. The Architect looked sickly and enfeebled. The Architect turned around and tried one more attack on Menzi.

Menzi swiftly grabbed the Architect by the throat and pushed him back onto a seat. He tied the Architect up so that it could not escape the seat. Menzi then quickly grabbed a helmet-like headset that was connected to the supercomputer.

The Architect fidgeted and shook trying to escape the seat in vain. Menzi ran over to a switch and pulled a lever. The section of the control room began to light up and the seat that the Architect was on shook violently. Sparks flew around the seat and the Architect shook manically.

The turbulence ended as quickly as it began. Menzi had just successfully uploaded the Architect's consciousness onto the Zeta Reticuli supercomputer. Menzi breathed a sigh of relief. He slowly walked up to the Architect's body, still strapped up to the seat.

Menzi aimed a photon rifle at the Architect's body. Menzi fired a shot that vaporised the Architect's body, as a way of making sure that the Architect's body had no body to return to in the flesh and bone, carbon-based universe.

The Architect's consciousness awoke in a white empty space. His consciousness looked around and saw nothing but white light. Suddenly a group of tall, ethereal authority figures surrounded him. He knew that he was surrounded by the manifest consciousnesses of the Zeta Reticuli.

"You days of ruling with an iron fist are over, Architect. You will never strike terror in the heart of another living thing again," said a booming voice from this group of consciousness manifest. The Architect let out a hellish scream as its consciousness was destroyed once and for all.

Meanwhile in the control room, Menzi's legs buckled, and he fell to his knees, relieved that the battle was over and that his plan had worked. He sobbed with joy as he put his Nommo blade away and wiped the sweat from his brow.

"Hey, Sheh! I did it. You helped me do it. I saved the universe!" Menzi said, halfway laughing. A robotic avatar walked up behind Menzi. "Yes, you did, Menzi. The cosmic brain could use some quick cleaning and repairs, of course, but you have saved us all. Well done," said Sheh.

Menzi sat in the control room with his face down and beamed a smile to himself, knowing that even though the universe remained broken and full of pain, it would live to hopefully heal itself.

Epilogue

Location: Andromedople the City of the Andromedans, one standard week later.

Innozia was in her imperial chamber preparing to address the Andromedan empire. She was still nursing some minor injuries from the battle she had just had with her sister's militia and the Mathra a standard week ago, but she had no time to fret about that.

She had just been coronated as the Queen of Andromeda after the passing of her sister Natiki in battle. However, instead of retreating to enjoy the spoils of being the queen of her own empire, Innozia believed that there was some important business for her and the empire to take care of.

She wore a mesmerising vantablack dress that shifted in its shape regularly. On her neck hung necklaces with charms that bore the faces of the previous queens of Andromeda, including her mother Oyo Seviv, her sister Natiki and her grandmother Sabursa.

Innozia applied cosmetic paint to her face that had the ability to change colour. She looked to the mirror in her chamber and smiled to herself. An Andromedan servant stood at her doorway waiting to report to the new queen.

"Your majesty, it is time for you to address the Andromedan Parliament. Your people are waiting," the servant said. Innozia looked to the servant and nodded. The newly crowned queen stood up and walked out of her chambers and into the passage.

Innozia arrived at a black shimmering wall. She could hear the large crowd of Andromedople aristocrats and parliamentarians murmuring to each other and speculating what she would announce to them. Suddenly she heard the voice of her herald, calling the gallery to attention.

"Andromedans here and across the cosmos. All rise to acknowledge your ruler and queen; The mother of peace and concord; the daughter of the ages; the joy and redemption of the universe; the love and consolation of all living things; your ruler and mine, Queen Innozia!" the herald extolled.

The black, shimmering wall that was in front of Innozia disappeared to reveal a hovering platform for the queen to step on. She stepped onto the platform, and it slowly descended down to the imperial seat that her mother, Queen Oyo, once sat on.

Once it got to the seat, Innozia stepped to the throne and assumed her position as ruler of one of the universe's most powerful empires as her subjects bowed in reverence. She took her seat and the entire gallery prostrated themselves before her.

The queen looked down, slightly nervous, knowing that what she was about to tell the gallery of Andromedan aristocrats would change the course of her empire forever and would likely ruffle feathers amongst the Andromedan elite. She nodded and proceeded to speak.

"Andromedans, I speak to you today with a full heart. In a very short space of time, you deployed me as leader of our imperial guard in a campaign against our enemies, you gave my departed mother a fitting burial, did the same with the body of my sister and welcomed me in grand triumph from a successful campaign. And I thank you for it. It has not been an easy journey to this throne for me and I would have much preferred that my mother were here to make these difficult decisions. But I come before you today firmly convinced that these decisions must be made," Innozia said.

The Andromedans listened attentively. Innozia's mind shifted to the peoples she had met on her last adventure and the impact they had on her and how she saw the cosmos. Innozia drew in a breath and continued.

"We have a proud tradition of expansion and conquest as Andromedans. Some in the imperial palace believed that this would continue forever. Other had become so accustomed to it that it bored them. But the universe is changing, and we can no longer determine our place in it based on our whims and wiles alone. Yes, the universe is changing and so should we," said Innozia.

The Andromedan parliamentarians were now whispering and murmuring among themselves, wondering what drastic change Queen Innozia would announce. Innozia prepared herself for dissent and proceeded.

"From now on, the Andromedan empire will cede all planetary, star system, and galactic territories that we have colonised and occupied over the eons. All planetary civilisations in these territories will also be granted their freedom with no conditions. As part of a commitment to rectifying our colonial history, we will also negotiate with these peoples as they tell us how we are to pay out reparations to them for all they have lost due to the Andromedan colonial project," Innozia said.

The murmurs got louder as the aristocrats of the Andromedan empire gasped in dismay and shock at what their queen had just said. Innozia looked down at the parliamentarians understanding that the reaction was decidedly negative.

"What is more, the Andromedan citizenship will henceforth be afforded to anyone who lives under the empire, and not just ethnic Andromedans. Too many peoples and lifeforms are loyal to Andromeda and have to go without the benefit of Andromedan citizenship. This changes today," Innozia said.

The murmurs and muttering were now shouts and heckling. Innozia raised her hand in a bid to restore order and quiet. The heckling still got louder. A pang of self-doubt sat in Innozia's chest, as she realised that the parliamentarians were defying her order to maintain their silence.

"How can this be?!" protested one Andromedan parliamentarian. "First, we give up land and planets and resources and now anyone can become an Andromedan? This is unheard of, my queen. It would be a grave mistake!" the parliamentarian fretted.

Innozia looked at the other parliamentarians and saw that they were arguing and panicking as they talked to and shook each other. She saw others gesturing in her direction mouthing insults to those around them.

"That is enough!" Innozia yelled. The Andromedan Parliament suddenly fell quiet. All of the parliamentarians in the house looked to Queen Innozia and no one dared to make a sound until she had her say.

"My campaign has taught me, with no ambiguity the horrifying ramifications of our colonial project. After having defeated the Mathra in war, I am now under no illusions that they would not have even existed had it not been for Andromeda. The more that we seek to extend ourselves the more oppressed people's hearts fill with hatred for us and the more we will have to look over our shoulders for fear of the consequences of what we have done to them. I say no more!" said Innozia.

"We have enough wealth to last us until the death of the last star in the sky. Why do we horde more when so many go without...when so many go without because of us? I will take this opportunity to remind the members that this is not a debate but a decree. We are withdrawing from our colonies; we are paying reparations to all colonised civilisations, and we are expanding Andromedan citizenship to all in our empire who wish to have it. My plans for these reforms will be announced in due course. And opposition or dissent will be viewed as treason. I have spoken and I call this house to rise," Innozia concluded.

The shocked parliamentarians still prostrated themselves before the queen as she left their presence. Innozia left her imperial seat and took to the hovering board, levitating back to the passage she came from.

Even though the newly crowned queen's heart was pounding from the thrill of what she had just done she wiped a tear of joy from her face as she ascended knowing that whether her decision was popular or not, she did the right thing.

Meanwhile on Kappess moon in the Pleiades

The traveling Pleiadian, Altanara, arrived back at Kappess moon in a small spaceship big enough for only one driver. He smiled as he arrived back. The sights were soothing for him as he saw the Pleiadians rebuilding after the devastation of the battle that occurred there just days ago.

Pleiadian brothers could be seen using telekinesis to lift boulders and bricks as they were rebuilding the sanctuary and its sacred temple. Taheeq turned out to look into the distance and saw that Altanara had just arrived.

Taheeq arrived to greet Altanara with a smile. "My Pleiadian brother. I am so happy to see you. I hope you travelled well and that you kept safe as the battle ensued," Taheeq said to his fellow Pleiadian. The two embraced and Taheeq took Altanara's luggage.

"Everything is good, brother Taheeq. I just had to come back and help my people rebuild. Apologies for not being here on time when the battle called for it. We have lost a lot in this period, and we needed every hand that we could get," Altanara said.

"Not to worry my bother. The work you did in visiting the Andromedan Parliament was more than enough. In fact, I hear that the Andromedan royal family may have softened its heart towards your appeals (*see Sirius Squad 2: Between Enemy Lines)," Taheeq said.

"It was the least that I could have done," Altanara said with a smile. As the two Pleiadians walked towards the site of the sanctuary, Altanara noticed the construction of the temple still being rebuilt took up more land space than the now destroyed sanctuary.

"What are you building over there? It seems like there is going to be a lot more on the site than just what was there before," Altanara inquired, pointing at a foundation where there was once a bed of flowers.

"We're creating an outpost for food there. We thought it would be a good idea to be more active in helping civilisations and lifeforms around the universe that were devasted by the war, or the Mathra, or Andromeda, anything, really," Taheeq explained.

Altanara nodded attentively. "Is this about what Tawa was saying before he died? Do you think he was right? Do you feel like we should have done more than just watch as the injustice took place?" Altanara asked Taheeq.

Taheeq paused as he looked up to the skies. "Tawa was wrong. He could not force the universe into prosperity as he hoped to. Mogori was a great leader, and we are certainly poorer without his wisdom. However, I believe many of us have grown weary of watching the universe suffer while we live in tranquillity. We are not here to force the universe into any ideal paradise that we think it ought to be, but we can do our bit to end suffering where we can. It feels better to get involved in the affairs of the cosmos by providing relief rather than picking up arms to fight," Taheeq responded.

Altanara looked to Taheeq and smiled. Taheeq smiled back and the two walked on to greet their other brothers from the sanctuary. While they did not know what the future held for the Pleiades, they knew that they had a wealth of wisdom to rely on as they worked to redefine their place in it.

Meanwhile on planet Nibiru, in the Sirius Star System

Menzi and Mogoma had just finished climbing up to the highest peak on planet Nibiru. Menzi was mesmerised by all that he saw on his first visit to the planet of his people. The metallic grey skies did not have any gloom to them, and the silver waves of the planet's back-to-back oceans amazed him.

The two Nommo each carried a surfboard in hand as they stood at the summit of a hill on one of the planet's floating islands. Menzi had suggested it to Mogoma as a hobby that could potentially catch on in Nibiru.

Menzi looked out at the view. "It's so beautiful. I expected it to be a feast for the eyes, sure, but this is beyond stunning," the young Nommo warrior said. Menzi looked out at the floating flowers in the air and the crashing waves that seemed to go on forever.

"That's right. This has been our home for eons, and it is your home too, young Nommo. You are always welcome here and you have as much right to be here as any other Nommo," Mogoma said to Menzi.

Menzi 's face turned serious. "I wish I could have gotten to know her," he said, lamenting the fact that Elder Amma died before he could get the chance to meet with her.

"The loss of our mother saddens me too. I hope you can at least find comfort in the knowledge that, in a very powerful way, she is always with you. When you travelled back to meet with the Nommo from earth's past, she was with you all the way," Mogoma said, offering comfort to Menzi.

Menzi smiled at Mogoma. His face turned pensive again. "Can I ask you a question? Does it bother you at all that I'm just going straight back to earth after this? Would it be better for me to just live here with the rest of the Nommo?" Menzi asked.

"Young Nommo, I want you to live where your heart will find fullness. That is where a Nommo belongs. Like I said, you are free to come here at any time. If your heart tells you to be on earth, then that is where you should be. After all, you should at least be there because that is where you placed the Positive Logos, correct?" Mogoma taunted with a laugh. Menzi softly laughed back.

"Left it in the capable hands of your earth brother, didn't you?" Mogoma asked rhetorically. The two smiled at each other. "Meanwhile, the Negative Logos will be safe right here on Nibiru. We have every confidence that you are up to the task of guarding the Positive Logos on earth," Mogoma reassured.

Menzi looked out into the distance and then turned to Mogoma. "Thank you, Mogoma. Thank you for everything. You were a mentor when I needed guidance. You believed in me more than I believed in myself. I could not have defeated the Architect without you," Menzi said.

Mogoma just smiled back and rubbed Menzi's shoulder. "You always had it in you," Mogoma said. "But if you don't mind me saying this, I thought we came here to surf, not to get sentimental," the older Nommo quipped.

The two Nommos laughed. They then looked out into the distance and proceeded to jump off the summit of the hill onto their surfboards. The two Nommo warriors slowly and gently glided into the water for a refreshing and relaxing surf, away from the troubles of any world.

THE END

About The Author

Khulekani Magubane is a journalist and author from Estcourt, KwaZulu Natal. He has been writing published books since 2004. He currently works in Cape Town as a journalist covering the political economy and developments in Parliament. He enjoys travelling, writing and storytelling. He has been invited to literary events including the 2014 Time of The Writer in Durban, the Cape Town Book Fair in 2012 and the Storymoja Book Festival in Nairobi, Kenya in 2015. As an author, he has been interviewed by various publications, television shows, radio segments and international magazines such as Netherlands-based Das Goethe and the International Journal of Environmental Research and Public Health.

About The Book

In the third and final instalment of the Sirius Squad trilogy, Menzi Gumede must dig deeper than he ever has before to find the strength and resolve to end the onslaught of the evil Mathra bandits who are on a mission to destroy the universe and remake it in their own image. He must also reckon with the brutal colonial history of the Andromedan empire which mirrors his own experience of living with the ramifications of the colonial project on a tiny blue planet called earth. In this exciting conclusion to his epic adventure, Menzi travels to the furthest stars in the sky, but learns about himself and his own world in the process. But he cannot forget that the fate of the universe lies in his hands.

Printed in the United States
by Baker & Taylor Publisher Services